The Chemistry Complication

Maggie Linn Sharpe

Paperback Edition ISBN-13: 979-8-9923370-7-5

eBook Edition ISBN-13: 979-8-9923370-8-2

Cover design by Maggie Linn Sharpe.

Edited by: Lily Luchesi, Partners In Crime Book Services

Also by Maggie

The Songbird Cafe Series

The Songbird Setup (Leena & Bailey)

The Boss Boycott (Annie & Eric)

The Marriage Meltdown (Jessie & Dan)

The Chemistry Complication (Cass & Griffin)

Beachville Springs

State of Grace (Meg & Hunter)

Author's Note

The Chemistry Complication includes a main character whose history includes childhood abuse at the hand of a parent as well as the neglect of her other parent, who has since passed. While the instances of abuse do not appear on page, there is mention of physical, mental, and emotional abuse.

Included in these instances is the control of food that resulted in an eating disorder for our main character. While her eating disorder is not active during this story and has been treated professionally, it and some of the after effects she experiences are mentioned.

If any of these topics are something you would find difficult to read, that's completely fine. Feel free to skip this one and rejoin us for our move to the small town of Beachville Springs. All of my books can be read as standalones, so you can pick up with the next series.

Never be afraid to protect your heart and your mental health!

xo, Maggie

For anyone who's been hurt by someone who was meant to protect you.

It was never your fault.

Contents

Chapter One

Cass

"It's fucking packed in here!" I shout, leaning close to my best friend, Meg.

"What?" she shouts back.

I roll my eyes, close to hitting my limit for people-ing. Between the crowds at the Arnold Sports Festival, where we spent our day, and this busy Short North bar, I've about had it.

"It's packed! I need some air!" I yell directly into Meg's ear. She nods, and we make our way out the front door. My ears ring in the relative quiet of the busy street. Columbus isn't a huge city, but this area is hopping tonight.

It's been unseasonably warm for early March in Ohio, so everyone is enjoying the escape from winter hibernation. Between the nicer weather and the crowds overflowing from the convention, the bars are slammed with people tonight. I take a deep breath of cool air and close my eyes for a moment, begging for the impending headache to fuck off.

"It was so stinking hot in there!" Meg huffs, waving at herself. She pulls her curly blonde hair up into a messy bun and fans the back of her neck. "It feels good out here."

"Do we want to go back in there or try somewhere else?"

"Kid-free weekend, Cassidee!" she yells with her arms in the air. "Mama wants to go somewhere we can dance!"

I laugh and shake my head at my oldest friend, the only one who could ever get away with calling me by my full name. Best friends since second grade, we grew up in the same tiny town in West Virginia, and both moved to Ohio for college; me at The Ohio State University, her at Ashland University. She can't resist the small-town vibe.

Even now, she lives in a dinky town about an hour from Columbus, in the opposite direction from Fort Starling, the medium-sized city where I live. We meet in the middle whenever we get a chance, but as a single mom, she doesn't get away much. I try to get over to Beachville Springs as often as I can get away since it's easier for me. I practically lived there when her husband, Gavin, passed away a couple of years ago.

Widowed at twenty-eight with a two-year-old, she needed a lot of help for a while. Kids aren't my favorite thing, but my "nephew," Beckett, is the exception. I'd do anything for that kid. He's the closest I'll ever come to having my own kids, so I've embraced my role as Aunt Dee Dee.

Meg's elbow nudging my arm pulls me out of my thoughts. "Look! There's a bar having an early 2000s dance party tonight! Let's go relive the seventh-grade dance where we memorized a choreographed dance to 'Get Low'! Please, Dee Dee?"

I let out a big sigh and pinch my nose. "Fine. But I'm not doing the dance if that song plays. I have limits, Margaret!"

"Ew, don't Margaret me. You sound like my mother."

"Well, stop calling me Dee Dee. Only Beck is allowed. You're already pushing it using my full name. Everyone else calls me Cass."

"Fine, fine," she says with an eye roll and a dismissive hand wave. She grips my shoulders and shakes me side to side and says in a whiny voice, "Let's go dance!"

I laugh and shake my head at her. Her bright blue eyes have taken on a crazy quality, so there's no point in fighting her on this. She needs this night out, and I won't be the one to stand in her way.

"Let's go," I say tiredly, waving my arm down the street toward our next stop.

"Yes!" Meg fist-pumps and takes off down the street, eyes still trained on her phone. I sigh and follow, keeping my eyes up to make sure she doesn't run into anything. "Oh! Zander's gonna meet us there! He'll do the dance with me!"

Meg shimmies her shoulders, and I huff another laugh. Zander is another transplant from our small town. We were always friendly with him growing up, since we were all devoted drama kids, but we bonded with him more once we got to college. He went to OSU with me, and it was there I realized we had way more in common than we thought. Our closed-minded town may not have kept him all the way in the closet as the only out bisexual kid in our class, but he definitely let his true personality shine more once we hit the freedom of college.

"LADIES!" we hear a booming voice call from down the street. Without even looking, I know it's Zander waiting for us in front of the bar.

"ZANDY!" Meg shouts back, and I laugh. He hates it when we call him that. It's a night for annoying nicknames, apparently. Meg takes off in a half-jog, half-stumble walk toward him. She definitely had more to drink than I did at the last bar. She throws her arms over his shoulders as he spins her around in a circle. Their ten-inch height difference makes it easy for him to lift her curvy body off the ground.

"How's my Meggy?" he says affectionately before setting her on her unsteady heels.

"Kid-free night, baby!" she shouts, throwing her arms in the air again.

Zander laughs and turns to give me a more laid-back hug.

"She's been hitting the vodka, hasn't she?" he murmurs in my ear.

"She's having a fun night. She deserves to let loose sometimes." I give Zander a sad smile, knowing we're both thinking about everything Meg's been through the last couple of years.

"On it. I'll take her to the dance floor; you bring baby girl a drink!" He links arms with Meg as we enter the bar, and they head straight to the dance floor, where the DJ is playing a dance remix of Rihanna's "Don't Stop the Music." I smile and make my way over to the bar.

I order a Diet Coke for myself, a beer for Zander, and a vodka cranberry for Meg before turning to face the dance floor while I wait. Meg and Zander are right on the edge of the crowd, dancing like idiots, and I can't help but smile at them. Meg's blonde curls are escaping the bun she put them in, and Zander looks like he should be on a runway somewhere with his stylish clothes and movie star looks. They're really bringing down resting bitch face vibes I usually like to put out. With a laugh, I turn to grab the drinks, tip the bartender well, and head out to join my crazy friends.

I'M AT THE BAR again, but this time for water for Meg. She's been hitting both the dance floor and the vodka cranberries hard. I'm way too sober for this, and if it were anyone else, I would have bailed an hour ago. I grab the waters from the bar and spin around, running right into a tall, suit-clad person.

"Well, fuck," the man says. "I thought I'd at least get a chance to speak to you before you threw your drink at me."

"I'm so sorry!" I look up into the face of one of the most handsome faces I've ever seen, smiling down at me. He's clean-cut, with dark hair swept to the side and gelled in place. The button-down shirt under his suit jacket is unbuttoned at the top, his tie pulled loose. He's pulling his wet shirt away from his chest as much as he can, but hasn't lost the glimmer of humor on his face.

"It's fine. It was hot in here, anyway." He shoots me another dazzling smile, and I almost lose my grip on the half-empty water glasses I still have clutched in my hands. I meet his grin with a scowl. I'm not the type of girl to be stunned by a pretty face, and the instant butterflies that just took flight in my stomach are pissing me off. I'd walk away saying nothing, but I did spill water on him, so I'm conflicted.

"Sorry again," I say politely, then start to walk away. He steps into my path. My scowl deepens, and his smile brightens even more.

"Actually, I was coming over here to ask if I could buy you a drink."

"No, thank you." I try to walk away again, and he steps into my path again. This pretty boy is asking for the rest of these waters to be thrown in his face.

"You did spill your drinks on my shirt. It's the least you could do." He smirks and raises his eyebrows as he pulls his very soaked shirt away from his chest again.

I blow out a big breath of air, feeling torn. I can tell him off, insist I don't owe him anything, but I'm intrigued. This man is *so* not my usual type. He looks like a golden retriever in a suit, whereas my taste leans more toward bearded, tattooed biker guys. But there's something intense in his expression that makes me want to stay.

Before I can make up my mind, Zander and Meg appear next to us. Meg is clearly gone, so I shove the water into her face.

"Drink, Meggy!"

"Ooo, I love drinkies! Oh, ew, it tastes like plain water!" She makes a disgusted face, crinkling her nose up, and I laugh.

"It is water; you're trashed. It's time to go." I turn to Mr. Suit. "Sorry, I've gotta get her home."

Zander chooses that moment to pipe up. "I've got her. You stay."

My eyes go wide. "It's okay, I can leave," I grit out through clenched teeth.

We have a silent argument with Zander, making big eyes and head gestures toward the handsome man waiting next to us, who watches with a look of fascination on his face. With my own facial expressions, I try to say I don't want to stay, but Zander can see through even my nonverbal bullshit.

Zander spins to face the guy, blocking my view of him. "Can I see some ID?"

"Zander!" I huff.

"No, if I'm leaving my bestie here in this bar with this beautiful hunk of Fiyero-looking man-candy, I'm at least gonna find out who we'll be investigating should you go missing!"

I roll my eyes. I've been taking care of myself for a long time and don't need Zander acting like my protective big brother, but I also know there is nothing I can say to stop his theatrics. The gorgeous guy chuckles good-naturedly and pulls out his wallet. He hands his ID to Zander, who snaps a quick picture of it before handing it back and linking his arm with Meg.

Zander gives me a quick kiss on the cheek and murmurs in my ear, "You better climb that man like a tree. The universe granted you a perfect specimen, and I'd better get a complete rundown of your sweaty night tomorrow at brunch!" He smacks me on the ass and escorts Meg out the door before I can say anything more.

With another stunning smile, the guy looks at me, still holding his ID in his hand. "Do you want to check it too?" he asks, offering me the card.

I shake my head, making a wild decision. "No. I don't want to know your name."

His eyebrows shoot up. "You don't want to know my name at all?"

"Nope. No names."

"So I can't know your name either?"

"No."

He nods his head and runs a hand along his chin, thinking it over before he leans in close to whisper in my ear, "Then how will you know what name to scream out later?"

My jaw drops, and I lean back sharply. I should probably be offended, but I can see the challenge in his eyes, and I can't help the wave of heat that overtakes me. He may look like a nice guy with the suit and haircut, sparkling smile shining, but the glint of heat in his eyes tells me he might have just enough bad boy in him to keep me interested. At least for one night.

I don't do more than one night.

He smirks as I stare him down, and I want to wipe it off his face, so I grab his tie in my hand and use it to pull him down so I can reach his ear. "I guess you'll just have to keep my mouth busy."

That did it.

He leans back to study me, heat flaring in his eyes, smirk gone. He swallows hard. "Drink?" He leans a head toward the bar.

"Lead the way, Slick."

He stops in his tracks. "Slick, huh? That's what you're going with?"

"Feels like it fits. Clean-cut guy like you. I'm sure you're used to talking girls out of their panties every weekend."

He raises his eyebrows, humor dancing in his eyes. "Whatever you say, Spitfire."

I bark out a laugh. Honestly, pretty spot-on for someone who's known me for two seconds. I like how he can already read me. Gives me hope I'll finish this night with an orgasm or two.

I follow him to the bar where I order a Jack and Diet, and he orders a scotch neat. We sit sipping for a beat before he scoots closer. The bar is so loud; we have to speak up to be heard.

"So, no names. Any other rules?"

"No details. I don't want to know where you live, what you do, or any other identifying information. Just an anonymous night of fun."

He sips his drink, giving me a slow nod.

"Any particular reason you want to stay anonymous? You're not married, are you?"

I huff a laugh. "Fuck no. I don't do complications. Are you married?"

"No, definitely not married." A strange expression crosses his face, but he shakes it away. "Okay then, Spitfire. Am I allowed to tell you I think you're the most fascinating woman I've ever met?"

"You've known me for ten minutes," I say with an exaggerated eye roll, doing my best to hide how pleased I am by his compliment.

"I said what I said," he says in a serious voice, his eyes locking on my own. I can't tell what color they are in the flashing strobe lights coming from the stage, but their intensity sends a shiver down my spine.

We finish our drinks at the same time. He starts to speak, but the song playing catches my attention.

"Ah, oh my god, I have to go dance," I yell out as I slide off the barstool.

"What?" he shouts, following me.

"This is my song. If it plays, I dance. I don't make the rules." I walk toward the dance floor, and he grabs my hand. At first, I think he's going to pull me back toward the bar or toward the door, but he surprises me when he pulls us to the dance floor.

"Then let's dance."

"Hips Don't Lie" has been my signature party song since college. Really, I've loved it since it started playing on the radio when I was in middle school. All my friends knew that if they played Shakira, I would come running. Blame it on the tiny amount of Puerto Rican heritage I have. Give me a Latin beat, and I will gladly shake my ass immediately.

It's a whole different vibe to have a strong, handsome man holding onto my hips from behind. Slick turns out to be an excellent dancer. Our bodies mold together as we sway and grind to the music. He's the perfect height to match my five-foot-nine frame. He has to be at least six-two, able to wrap me in his arms. He sings along to the music directly in my ear, making chills run down my spine. We stay out on the floor for several more songs until we're sweaty and I'm dying for a drink.

Reading my mind, Slick leans down and asks, "Do you want a drink? Or do you want to get out of here? My hotel is only a few blocks away."

Hotel. So, he's not local. I ignore the disappointment flooding me. That's weird. I don't double-dip, so it shouldn't matter if he's not from here. Probably just in town to sell something at the Arnold. It's better this way.

With my mind made up, I nod and grab his hand, walking toward the door.

"Let's go."

Chapter Two

Cass

THE SHORT WALK TO his hotel in the frigid March air cools us down from our time on the dance floor. He's in one of the fancier boutique hotels downtown, and we manage to keep some distance between us on the short walk.

The lobby is mostly deserted this late at night, and we hurry across the chic space. When we hit the elevator, the heat rises between us again. We barely make it to his room before his hands are on me, and I'm tugging at his clothes.

Our lips crash together, and he presses me into the wall next to the door, lifting me off my feet. I wrap my legs around him, burying my hands in his hair as he licks and bites a path along my lower lip, which quickly travels down my neck.

He carries me to the bed and tosses me onto the plush surface, where I land with a bounce. A light laugh escapes from my mouth, surprising me. Slick shoots me a triumphant grin, like he's proud of himself for getting me to laugh. The tension crackles between us as we lock eyes for a long moment.

This suddenly feels intimate in a way I usually avoid, so I decide to get us back on track by pulling the lightweight black sweater I wore to the convention over my head, followed quickly by the lace bralette I had underneath. Slick's not smirking now. His eyes are dark with heat as he takes in my topless form.

I've always been proud of my breasts. They're big enough to be a full handful without being so heavy they've drooped with age, at least not yet. I take advantage of his attention by cupping them in my hands, rolling the nipples between my fingers. Slick lets out a groan as he watches me.

"Fuck, you're gorgeous. I can't believe you were hiding those tits under there. I need to taste them." He pounces, pinning my back to the bed as he kisses down the center of my chest. He uses both hands to knead and squeeze both breasts before lowering his head and drawing a nipple into his mouth.

He gives it a suck before biting down hard. It's like there's a live wire running from my nipple straight to my clit, and I arch off the bed as he repeats the motion on the other side. He doesn't let up with his kissing and nips along my boobs as he trails a hand down to the button of my jeans, popping them open.

"Are you wet for me, Spitfire?" His fingers graze the outside of my satin thong, which is indeed already soaked through. "Is all this for me?"

"Yes, fuck, I'm so ready," I gasp as his fingers nudge my underwear to the side. He runs the tip along my drenched slit, and I hiss as my hips punch forward. I want him closer. I want him inside me. "Please."

"Please, what? Talk to me, Spitfire. Tell me what you want."

"Touch me. Now."

"You got it." He leans back and yanks at my jeans, shimmying them down my hips, taking my thong, socks, and boots with them. "Let's get rid of these."

I'm completely bare for him when I suddenly realize he's fully dressed. Part of me is turned on by the disparity. The unbalanced power dynamic of him still wearing his suit and me being stark naked is potent, but I want to see what he's got going on under the strait-laced clothes. I sit up and start yanking on his shirt.

"You're wearing too many clothes."

He chuckles and helps me get rid of his jacket, shirt, and tie. He looks good enough to eat. His shoulders and chest show the definition of someone who works out regularly, but not so cut to make me think he lives at the gym. He turns to kick his shoes off and graces me with the sight of some stunning ink trailing up his ribcage and around to his shoulder blade. Looking more closely, he's got tattoos trailing both sides of his ribs and along his inner biceps.

Maybe he's not the slick, strait-laced nice guy after all.

I reach to pop the button on his pants, pushing them down along with the boxer briefs he wears. His dick bounces up, already hard, with the smallest bead of pre-cum lingering at the tip. I swipe it with my thumb as I wrap my hand around him and give him a slow pump.

Slick drops his head back and groans. He lets me play for a minute before he pushes me back down onto the bed. He kneels between my legs as he tears open the condom wrapper he must have grabbed while I was studying his tattoos.

Once he's fully sheathed, he lowers down, pressing his body against mine. He lines up his cock with my entrance, and he kisses me again, hard, right as he pushes his way inside. It's a tight fit, and he goes slow, stretching me around his thick erection.

"Oh fuck. You're so fucking tight. You're gonna make me lose my mind."

I let out a breathy moan as he bottoms out. He waits a second before pulling almost all the way out and slamming home again. My back arches and my hips buck, trying to keep him buried. I meet him thrust for thrust as he picks up the pace. I'm already so close, as my pussy clenches around him.

"Let go, Spitfire. Come for me."

His words send me over the edge with a long moan, and I shatter around him as he keeps the pace steady, never letting up. I breathe deeply for just a moment as I come down from my orgasm. His unflagging pace sparks another wave of heat low in my belly, and I'm startled to find the current rising again. I chase the feeling, writhing and thrusting under him.

He pulls out, and before I know what's happening, he's flipped me over, ass in the air, and my elbows resting on the bed. He slides back inside me, and the new angle is delicious. I push back into him on every thrust, our moans mixing in the air.

"I'm right there. Come with me, give me one more." He groans into my spine as he loops his arm around me. The second he touches my clit, I detonate again. My vision goes white, and all I can think about is the violent pleasure coursing through my body, making every muscle contract and spasm.

We collapse onto the bed side by side, both breathing hard. We lie in companionable silence for several minutes before he stands to dispose of the condom, and I gather my clothes.

"That was fantastic," I call out as I'm sliding my thong up my hips.

"What are you doing?" He's leaning in the doorway to the bathroom, watching me pull my bralette back on.

"Getting dressed. I should head out."

"Why don't you stay for a bit? My buddy was telling me about a cookie place with late-night delivery." I keep getting dressed as I consider what he's saying. He's clearly not from around here if he didn't already know we have Insomnia Cookies nearby. I'm leaning toward staying, but I'm not ready to give in yet.

"I'm pretty sure I said this was a one-time thing," I say casually as I pull my jeans up.

"Actually, I think you said one night. And if you'd like to take a look out the window, you'll see the night is not over."

"Are you a lawyer or something?"

"Ah ah, you said no details."

I huff a laugh and roll my eyes. He stalks closer to me, still wearing only his black boxer briefs. He loops his arms around my hips, pulling me flush against him. I can feel my resolve breaking as warning bells chime in my head. This feels too good.

"We could get dessert, build up some energy for round two?" he murmurs in my ear.

I lower my head to his chest, and he rests his chin on my head. The embrace is intimate and comfortable. More reasons for me to hightail it out the door. This man could be addictive. The smart thing to do would be to gather my things and say goodbye to him.

"Alright, Slick, order the damn cookies."

What can it hurt to do the dumb thing for once?

"So when did 'Hips Don't Lie' become your signature song? There has to be a story there," Slick mumbles tiredly into my shoulder. I chuckle softly as I snuggle further under the covers.

What started with my sticking around for cookies and extra sex has turned into an entire night of doing things I *don't do*. I don't stay for dessert. I don't stay for third, fourth, and fifth orgasms. I don't shower with men I've just met, or any men for that matter. And I most certainly do not cuddle, but here we are.

The most surprising thing is how *not* weird the entire night has been. I keep waiting for it to turn awkward. For my panic to set in, forcing me to bail. But it hasn't happened yet. Ignoring all of my usual barriers and hangups has somehow felt comfortable and fun.

Right.

Slick has his arm wrapped around my waist, his breath tickling my neck as we take turns asking random questions, our pace slowing as we get sleepier. We've stuck to the rules I set earlier in the night. I don't know his real name, where he lives, or what he does for work. He doesn't know any identifying details about me. But in some ways, we know each other so much better. Learning minor details in our efforts to ignore the big ones.

I know he got the scar at the bottom of his chin in a childhood game of cops and robbers. His friend handcuffed him behind his back, just like on TV. His brother was already pretending to be dead on the floor, and Slick tripped, landing on the hardwood floor with no way to catch himself. The incident resulted in a trip to the ER, seven stitches, and a grape popsicle. He said he still teases his brother about tripping him from time to time.

It hasn't all been lightweight conversation, either.

He knows I keep a secret stash of snacks in my nightstand to make sure I don't go to bed hungry. I told him my mom was weird about food. I was a late bloomer, not reaching my full height until junior year. Until then, I had been on the heavier side, prompting my mother's obsession with my weight and food intake. He knows about the years of therapy to help heal the eating disorder she left me with.

I didn't go into all the details of my fucked-up relationship with my mother, like the way she used withholding food as a weapon, but I'm not sure I've ever told anyone besides my therapist about my snack drawer. No one sleeps in my house but me, so no one has seen it to question me on why I keep Cheez-its, Red Vines, and Zebra Cakes by my bed.

"You awake?" he murmurs, snapping me out of my thoughts.

"Yeah, sorry, zoned out. 'Hips Don't Lie'? Umm, well, I can distinctly remember the first day I heard it. I was like ten or eleven and—"

"Wait, ten or eleven? How old *are* you?" His voice sounds mildly panicked.

"I'm twenty-nine. I'll be thirty this summer."

"Oh. I guess it *is* about twenty years old. I was solidly in college when it came out."

"College? How old are *you*?" I ask with a laugh. I had already figured out he's older than me.

"I turned forty in January."

Ten years' difference. It's both a big age gap and nothing at all. Especially considering I'll never see him again after tonight. The thought leaves an unexpected lump in my throat. I swallow hard to clear it.

"Why does forty sound so much older than thirty?" I ask teasingly.

"Hey, now!"

"You're what? Gen X? Oh my god, are you a boomer?" He pinches my side, and I actually giggle. *Giggle.* There's another thing we can add to the list of things I only do under the spell of this man. A fact I'm sure I'll analyze to death when I'm back in the safety of my comfort zone.

"I'm a millennial, thank you very much," he huffs with a laugh.

"Maybe an elder millennial," I mumble, and he pinches me again. I laugh and snuggle closer to him.

We lapse into a companionable silence, and we must both fall asleep because the next thing I know, the light in the room has changed. Slick has rolled onto his back, no longer holding me. I listen to his slow, deep breaths for several minutes, debating whether I should stay until morning or sneak out now.

If I stay, I'll have to deal with the morning-after awkwardness. Or worse, the morning after won't be awkward, and he'll ask for my real name. My number. The panic that had been suspiciously absent all night floods my body, and I slip quickly from the bed. I gather my clothes and dress as quietly as I can.

I take one last look at Slick. Give myself one last chance to change my mind. But for the first time of the night, I stick to what I don't do.

I don't stay.

Chapter Three

Griffin

Three Months Later

"MELLIE! YOUR MOM'S HERE, let's go!" I yell up the stairs. Drew, my nine-year-old son, is already out in the front yard talking my ex-wife's ear off about what he did during the musical theater day camp he's been going to while I'm working. Thank goodness Fort Starling has a decent community theater, with all kinds of programming. The summer camps saved my ass.

Mellie, on the other hand, has been home with me. She turned thirteen this spring and insisted she was too old for "baby camps." She turned her little nose up in her now standard facial expression of disgust and disdain. Between the divorce, the move to Fort Starling, and official teenager status, she pretty much hates everything right now.

"Mellie! Come on!" I shout again. A loud stomping noise precedes her down the stairs, and I tense for battle.

"I don't see why I even have to go," Mellie whines. "I stay here with you all the time."

"You have to go because your mom wants to spend time with you. And I'm going out with Uncle Bailey."

The eye-roll my daughter sends me makes my jaw clench. What happened to my sweet little princess? This sulky creature looks like her, with her mother's long golden hair and my hazel eyes. But the scowl on her face is a new feature.

"Mom doesn't care about me," she grumbles.

"That is not true, and you know it. I know things have been hard for you, moving like this, but your mom loves you more than anything."

"Not more than her stupid new job," she says with a defiant lift to her chin.

"Amelia Grace Turner. Your mom has worked her ass off to get where she is in her career, all while making sure you have everything you could ever need. You have no idea the things she's done for you, for our family. Moving so she could have her dream job is the absolute least we could do for her. If I catch you disrespecting your mother, the phone you're so attached to will be gone."

She stares me down with her arms crossed.

"On that note, you ready to go, Mellie?" my ex-wife, Nessa, says behind me. I didn't hear her come in during my tirade. Mellie picks up her backpack with a huff and stomps out the front door, slamming it behind her.

I follow her and lean out the door to yell as loudly as I can, "I love you, Mellie Grace! Have a good weekend!"

Her shoulders hunch, and she looks around the empty yard for anyone who might have heard. "Dad," she whines before throwing herself into Nessa's car.

I chuckle before turning to Nessa. She has a smirk on her face as she grabs Drew's backpack. "Drew, baby, go on out to the car. I want to talk to Daddy for a bit."

"Okay, Mom!" Drew launches himself at me. "Are you gonna be okay without us, Dad?"

I huff a laugh. It's been a long-ass week, and I will be just fine with some peace and quiet, but I don't say that to my tender-hearted boy. "I'll miss you guys, but I'll be okay."

He gives me another squeeze and a solemn head nod. "You can call me if you need me."

"Thanks, buddy," I say, ruffling his blonde hair.

He bounces out the door and down the front walk to join his sister in the car. As soon as he's out of earshot, Nessa and I burst out laughing.

"Oh my God, how did he end up so sweet?" she says through laughs. "He didn't get it from me."

"Maybe he's siphoning it from his sister somehow? Mellie has gotten a lot less sweet lately."

Nessa chuckles and shakes her head. "Nah, it's the payback for how I was at her age. I'm pretty sure my mom would tell you I deserve anything our girl can dish out."

"Okay, but what did I do to deserve it?"

"Sorry, man, you're collateral damage." She wipes a stray tear from her eye and loops her hair behind her ears. Beautiful and put together as usual with her long, shiny hair and crystal blue eyes. I study her for just a moment, trying to find an ounce of the attraction I once had for her. I'm both relieved and sad to find it still missing.

Was it really ever there? It had to be, right? For us to date for years, get married, and have two kids together, there had to have been a spark at one point, right?

Fuck. My mind has been a mess ever since I spent the night with a tall, dark mystery girl who vanished before I woke up. The electricity I experienced with her from the second I saw her from across the crowded bar was unlike anything I've ever felt. How can that even be possible?

"I'd ask how the week's been, but I'm gonna guess I just got a preview?" Nessa raises her eyebrows, humor dancing in her eyes.

"Yep, Mellie's been a snarky mess of attitude and eye rolls, and Drew's been his happy little self. He loves the theater camp. I think we're gonna need to find something—anything—Mellie's interested in. I hate her sitting alone in this house stewing all week while I'm working."

Nessa sighs, pinching the bridge of her nose. "You're right. Getting her to be willing is the trick. She certainly won't agree to anything if I suggest it, now that I'm public enemy number one." Her chuckle is laced with pain this time.

"She'll come around, Ness." I reach out and pull Nessa into a hug. "It's an adjustment. Once school starts and she makes some friends, she'll hate us less for making her move."

Nessa blows out a big breath, tears filling her eyes. "I know. I just feel so guilty. The divorce was my idea. Moving here was my idea."

"Hey. I may have fought you on the divorce at first, but you were right. We were roommates with kids. And I won't let you feel bad about taking your dream job. Mellie will understand someday."

"Thanks, Griff." She wipes under her eyes and puts on her corporate badass face. "I'd better get out there before she decides to poison my water bottle."

I huff a laugh. "You can remind her that I will take her phone away if she's not nice."

Nessa laughs and offers me a wave before heading back to her car. I stand at the door and watch my family drive off. It's gotten easier over time, but there's still something so bittersweet about my free weekends. Sure, I get to do whatever I want. Sleep in, total control of the TV, no one to feed or discipline, but fuck is it lonely without them.

Luckily, tonight, I'm meeting my brother Bailey at his fiancée's bar for open mic night. I'll get to meet any of their friends I haven't met yet. Hopefully, I will solidify myself as part of their friend group. Maybe I could even meet someone to share some of these lonely weekends with. I haven't been with anyone since my wild night in Columbus. Someone new could help erase those images from my brain and the chokehold they've had on me since.

With that thought, I take off up the stairs to change clothes and get ready for a fun night out. This is exactly what I need to take my mind off my empty house and the dark brown eyes that have haunted me since March.

"There he is!"

My little brother, Bailey, comes over and pulls me into a bro hug right as I enter the Songbird Café and Bar, barely letting me get a look around the large open space before dragging me over to the bar where his fiancée, Leena, waits with some of their friends.

Bailey's six years younger than me, but we could almost pass for twins. Or at least we could if he wasn't so ripped from his job as a major league pitcher. The group is laughing at a story a tall blonde guy is telling. I think his name is Eric. We met a while back when I hung out at Bailey's best friend, Dan's, house who I see further down the bar with his wife, Jessie. I hope they're working through the rough patch they've been having, but I haven't heard an update lately.

"Hey, Griffin," Leena says, smiling at me as I duck to give her a hug in her seat. Her fiery red hair is down in soft curls tonight. "I think you've met everyone but Annie here." She motions to a light-brown-haired woman sitting between her and Eric. Annie gives me a wave. I'm about to reach out to shake her hand when Leena interrupts.

"Oh, and Cass!" Leena looks down the length of the bar over my shoulder.

Behind me, I hear a quiet but sharp whisper, "Oh, fuck." Chills instantly go down my spine, and I already know who's standing behind me.

I turn around, and there she is. My Spitfire. Dark brown hair, almost black, brushes the tops of her shoulders. Piercing dark eyes go wide as she studies my face, panic dancing in them. The black tank top she's wearing shows off the tattoos along her collarbone and shoulder. Tattoos I spent long minutes tracing with my tongue, hand fisted in her hair, her moans ringing in my ears. I frown as I remember waking up to an empty bed. No note, no trace of the dark beauty I spent a wild, intimate night with.

I clear my throat and step toward her. The desire to run is clear as day on her face. I offer her my hand to shake, and she takes it. "Cass, was it?

I'm Griffin." I can't quite keep the simmering anger out of my voice. I'm still pissed she left after everything we shared that night.

Never did I have such an intense night with a woman. Our connection was instant and powerful, and she walked away like it was nothing. I fell asleep planning to get her number in the morning. Her real name. I had visions of seeing her again once we were all moved and settled. But she vanished, and I haven't been able to get her out of my head.

The same spark from three months ago shoots up my arm, and we stand staring, our hands gripped together. The tension between us is almost unbearable, and I can sense my brother and his friends watching us with interest and confusion.

She murmurs empty pleasantries and makes her retreat. I excuse myself to the restroom. I need a minute to collect myself.

I debate leaving, but I don't want to give up my night out with Bailey and his friends. I'm trying to build a life here. I can't let a one-night stand derail the plan. And that's what we were. Spitfire—Cass—made sure we wouldn't be more with her rules and the way she disappeared.

I stare at my reflection in the small bathroom. *I can do this.* I can let it go and act normal around her. She's not the first one-night stand I've had in my life. She won't be the last. Now she's just the bartender at my brother's fiancée's bar. Who cares if the chemistry is still insanely strong between us? I can ignore it.

Fuck. Even in my head, it all sounds like bullshit.

I join Bailey back at the bar, and he hands me a beer. Leena and their other friends are engrossed in picking out songs to sing for open mic. I can tell they're doing their best not to stare at me. They clearly discussed my interaction with Cass while I was in the bathroom.

"You good, man?" Bailey asks in a quiet tone.

"Yeah, I'm fine," I lie.

I can see him about to call me on the lie, but I'm not discussing this with him here. Not where she could overhear us. Especially since I'm not sure how I feel about it all. I do my best to tell him telepathically I'm not interested in talking about it. He studies me for a long moment, then nods. He'll drop it for now, but I know he's not gonna let it go.

I do my best to join in the conversation. I'm hyperaware of Cass moving around the bar. She sits and hangs out with Leena and the girls for a while since she's got another bartender with her. I hear snippets of them planning a baby shower for Jessie, who's due in November.

Eric and I chat about the physical therapy practice that he owns with Annie. He's a friendly guy who tells funny stories about his patients and some of the pro baseball players he works with on my brother's team, the Fort Starling Flash.

Even as I carry on conversations with Bailey and his friends, I can't keep my focus from Cass, my eyes tracking her every time she moves to get someone a drink. I find out through the night that she's not just another bartender. She's the general manager, Leena's right hand in running this whole place.

I'm never gonna escape her here.

I finally decide to call it a night after some of our group disappear. I cross the street to the public parking lot where I left my car, only to find Cass reaching for the handle of her own, a newer-looking SUV.

She spots me over her shoulder and freezes. For a second, I think she's gonna get in her car and drive away, but she turns to face me.

"Hey," she says carefully, like she's not sure what to say to me.

"Hey, Spitfire," I murmur when I get close enough.

She winces. "Please don't call me that."

The anger that had cooled over the last few hours flares back to life. "Why not? Thought it was the only name I could call you."

She puffs out a breath. "Well, now you know my real name."

"I could have known your real name months ago if you hadn't taken off."

"I know. It's why I left. I don't do the long-term thing. It was better to just... go." She shrugs, awkwardness filling the space between us.

"Without a word. You just vanished. I woke up alone, wondering where the fuck you went."

"Yeah, well, I assumed I'd never see you again. I thought I'd save us an awkward morning after," she snaps.

"Worked out really well," I say sarcastically, not quite ready to let my agitation go yet.

She sighs and pinches the bridge of her nose. "Look, Griffin, it was three months ago. It was one night. It's best if we let it go. We're clearly going to see each other a lot since you're Bailey's brother. Let's just..." She swallows hard and studies her shoes, unable to look at me. "Let's pretend it didn't happen."

I stare her down until she looks up at me. When our eyes finally meet, it knocks the wind out of me, and the atmosphere thickens. Her lips part, and I know she feels it too. I move close to her, reveling in the way she has to tip her head back ever so slightly to look at me.

"How am I supposed to pretend it didn't happen when I can't stop thinking about that night? When I can still hear the way you gasped and moaned when I was buried deep inside of you?" I can see the heat in her eyes. I know she's picturing it, remembering the chemistry between us. I also see in her eyes the moment she snaps her guard back into place, a concrete wall sliding into place.

Impenetrable.

She clears her throat and steps back. "Let it go, Griffin," she says quietly before getting into her car and driving away.

I watch as her taillights disappear down the street. She's right. We should pretend it didn't happen. I should let it go.

But I'm not sure I can.

Chapter Four

Cass

"OKAY, TIME FOR YOU to fucking spill."

Leena's voice startles me from the other side of the bar from the spot I'm scrubbing. "What do you mean?"

"I tried to let it go. I tried not to pry, knowing you hate when people dig into your personal life, but I've been watching you with Griffin for weeks, and now you're about to scrub a hole into the bar top. So fucking spill already!" She blows out a frustrated breath, and I stare her down. But Leena just stares back; she's not gonna let this go. She's almost as stubborn as I am.

"Ugh, fine." I groan and reach behind me for a bottle of Maker's. I pour myself a shot and slam it back. I tilt my face up to meet Leena's wide eyes. "I had a one-night stand with Griffin in Columbus in March. It was... intense. I thought I'd never see him again. Except here he is. All. The. Time. I wanted to pretend it didn't happen, but Griffin... disagrees. So there's all this tension every time we interact, and it's making me grumpy."

Leena's jaw drops open, and her mouth opens and closes a few times before she lets out a bark of laughter. "I'm sorry. I'm sure it's not funny to you. But... 'of all the gin joints,' amiright?" She snickers some more into her Diet Coke, and I roll my eyes. "Well, fuck, that's not what I expected."

"Same."

It was the last thing I expected when I showed up to work a few weeks ago for open mic night and found the single one-night stand I can't get out of my head there at the bar. Finding out he's my best friend/boss's soon-to-be brother-in-law? Discovering he's divorced with two kids? Yeah, no, none of this was on my bingo card for this year.

"So, have you talked to him much? Other than the tense weirdness I saw yesterday?" Leena asks. "He's been in here every other week since that first time. Probably when Nessa has the kids."

"We had a conversation the first night he was here in the parking lot. Since then, there have been little comments here and there. Compliments, or he'll bring up something we discussed the night we met. Basically, just him showing that he's *not* pretending it didn't happen like I wanted."

It's been a special sort of hell having him here in the bar. The Songbird Café and Bar has been my safe space for the last few years. I wasn't sure where I was gonna go after I finished my MBA. I was just sure I wasn't going home. When Leena called with the idea for me to manage the bar she was opening, I jumped on it.

Now, after four years, it seems like home. Which reminds me...

"Hey, I wanted to talk to you about something, actually." Leena's eyebrows wing up at my change in tone. "My landlord is selling the house, and I have to move by the end of the month. I was wondering if I could move in upstairs? You can take the rent out of my paycheck. It makes more sense for me to live here since I'm already here so much."

Leena's nodding before I even finish. "Of course you can move in. Jessie's all moved out, so it's open for you. And I'm not taking rent out of your pay, it's n—"

"I don't want a handout, Leens," I cut her off.

"It's not a handout. You do so much here, and I'm sure I don't pay you nearly enough. And if you're living here, there's an extra peace of mind that the building is being taken care of. Seriously, you're doing me a favor by moving in here. You're not paying."

Recognizing Leena's no-bullshit tone, I let it drop there. "Thanks. I figure I'll move in slowly. I don't have to be out of my house until the 30th, so I can use the next few weeks to get everything over here. Most of the furniture stays with the house, so it won't be a big deal."

"Well, if you need any help, I know a guy with a truck." She winks at me. It's a running joke that Bailey ends up helping everyone move because he owns a pickup truck. It's extra ridiculous because, as a professional baseball player, he could easily hire movers or refuse, but he helps every time.

"I doubt I'll need to use Bailey's moving services, but I'll let you know."

"Now, back to you and Griffin," she says with a smirk as I groan and lower my head to the bar top. "Yeah, you're not getting out of playing twenty questions with me on this whole thing."

"One question."

"Ten."

"Three."

"Five," she says sternly.

"Ugh, fine." I get up and pour myself a Jack and Diet and get Leena a gin and Sprite. It's five o'clock somewhere.

"Okay, first question. How did you not put together that our Griffin was the same one you met in March? I saw your face. You were shocked to see him. You didn't think for one second, 'Maybe they're the same Griffin'?"

I keep my eyes locked on the bar when I confess, "I didn't know his name."

"You didn't know his name? You went home with a guy without knowing his name? Or did you do it in a bar bathroom?"

"Are these your official questions?" I ask with a sip of my drink.

"Of course not. Just... elaborate, please."

I sigh. "I didn't let him tell me his name or any identifying details. He didn't know any of mine. Zander took a picture of his driver's license before he and Meg left the bar. I felt safe enough with him to go back to his hotel without learning his name." I shrug and fiddle with my drink glass some more.

I can feel Leena's gaze on the side of my face, but I don't look up at her.

"Hmm, next question. How was it?" I snap my head to look at her, eyes wide. She hurries to clarify. "I don't want the play-by-play details. He *is* gonna be my brother-in-law, but like, was it a standard one-night stand, hit it and quit it sort of thing?"

I blow out another big breath. I might as well be honest with her. It may even help me figure out why I can't seem to move past it. "It was... more intense. I usually bail quickly after sex, but, uh, with Griffin... I stayed."

"You stayed? Like all night?"

"Long enough to fall asleep. I snuck out when I woke up a few hours later." Leena winces, and a pang of guilt hits me. Griffin seemed pretty pissed, even months later, that I left without a word. "It was shitty to bail without saying anything, but I already pushed my boundaries a lot. I needed to get out. I thought it would be better this way."

"Next question. Why didn't you want to know his name? It's not your usual style, right?"

I shrug. "It was a spur-of-the-moment decision. He tried to introduce himself, and I stopped him. It was instinct," I lie. I don't want to analyze why I didn't want to know Griffin's name with Leena right now. She lets out a hum and stares into her drink for a couple of long minutes. When she looks up at me, her face is full of serious concern. I expected her to give me crap for all of this, but now she's making me nervous with how seriously she's taking it.

"Alright, last question. I'll let you off with four, and honestly, you don't even need to answer this one out loud. I just want you to think about it." She waits and raises her eyebrows at me.

I swallow hard and nod at her.

"Do you think possibly the reason you did things differently that night, the reason you didn't want to know his name, the reason you broke your own rules, was because the connection you and Griffin have is strong and you were scared? Do you think you bailed in the middle of the night, not because it's 'what's best' but because you were freaked out by how right things feel between you?"

I don't have an answer, and I think Leena knows it. Just thinking about the things she's asking gives me a cold sweat. I'd say she probably hit the nail on the head. She pats my hand and slides down from her stool.

"I'm here if you need to talk, babes."

She heads out the front door, leaving me in the near-empty bar to contemplate the bomb she dropped on me.

LIKE CLOCKWORK, GRIFFIN SHOWS up at the Friday night open mic. He and Bailey sit at the bar when I come out with a tray of clean glasses. It's still early, and open mic hasn't started yet.

"Hey, Cass!" Bailey calls out in his friendly, golden retriever way.

"Bailey," I deadpan back at him, not giving him even a hint of a smile. It only makes him grin bigger. We're actually really good friends, but Bailey gets a kick out of my pretending I still don't like him. Our own little inside joke that developed while he was busy winning the heart of my best friend.

Griffin scoffs under his breath, and I turn my gaze to him. He looks so good in his green plaid button-down shirt that brings out the green in his hazel eyes. The dark beard with just a hint of grey he's let grow in gives him a dangerous, older guy vibe, only heightened by the heat lingering in his eyes as his gaze travels over me. I would not have nicknamed him Slick if he looked like this the night we met.

"Griffin," I say in my most polite, deadpan tone. I do my best not to let him affect me. "Can I get you guys drinks?"

"We'll take a couple of beers whenever you get the chance," Bailey answers. "Oh! Here, I brought you a burger and fries. I know the rules." I let myself smirk at the bag from Five Guys he hands across the bar.

"What rules?" Griffin asks, watching our interaction closely.

"I don't bring Five Guys into the bar without bringing Cass some," Bailey says through a bite of his burger. "It also applies to Taco Bell, Piada, and..." he looks over at me for help.

"Bibibop," I remind him.

"Right! I have a note on my phone with her order for all of those." He smiles at me, and I roll my eyes back at him.

Griffin's gaze goes back and forth between us like he's trying to figure out our relationship. I'm sure it looks strange from the outside.

"So, I heard you're joining the sisterhood of the Songbird apartment?" Bailey asks around a mouthful of fries.

"What are you talking about?" I ask, confused.

"You're moving into the apartment here, right?"

"Yeah, so?"

"So you're up next for your happily ever after!"

Griffin chokes on a sip of beer as I stare Bailey down. Bailey stares right back. I'm suddenly wondering exactly what Bailey knows, but I don't let anything show on my face. I give Bailey a look that says I think he's an idiot, and I'm not dignifying it with a response.

"What do you mean?" Griffin finally breaks the silence, shooting us both confused looks.

Bailey lets his grin shine through, breaking our stare down. "The last three ladies to live in the apartment got together—or back together in Jessie's case—with their partners while living there. Cass is up next!"

"I'm guessing Leena lived up there when you guys met?" Griffin asks, putting together the backstory for our friend group. "You said Jessie, who's the third?"

"Annie. She lived up there when she moved back from Chicago and before she moved in with Eric," Bailey explains with a waggle of his eyebrows. "That apartment has seen some things."

"Noted." Griffin is back to staring at me. Studying me. The heat of his gaze follows me as I move away to pull my food out of the bag. It gives my hands something to do so I don't have to focus on how his eyes on me make waves of heat flood my body. We're not doing this.

"Guess I'll be the one to break the streak," I say lightly. "I don't do happily ever after." I let my eyes meet Griffin's then. Instead of looking disappointed, warned, all I see is a challenge glinting back at me. Fuck.

"Anyway, thanks for the food, Bail," I say before retreating into the kitchen, unable to stand being this close to Griffin for another second. Leena's questions ring through my head as I climb the stairs to the still mostly empty apartment.

Why do I still feel so pulled toward him? How can I make it go away?

What would it be like to give in?

Chapter Five

Griffin

"ARE YOU GONNA TELL me what's going on there?" Bailey asks good-naturedly as I stare down the doorway Cass disappeared into.

"Nope." I take a big bite of my burger, knowing he's not gonna leave it there.

"Come on!" Bailey whines like only a younger brother can. "I got a bit of the story from Leena, but I want to hear your side."

My eyes snap to him. "What did Leena tell you?" I thought Cass would have kept everything to herself with the way she's trying to act like it didn't happen.

"Nuh-uh, I'm not telling you what I know until you spill the tea, big brother."

"Spill the tea?" I ask with eyebrows raised.

"Between hanging with Mellie and the young guys on the team, I'm full of Gen Z lingo. Wait, is it Gen Alpha?"

I roll my eyes and take another bite, but I notice Bailey still watching me out of the corner of my eye. He's not gonna drop it, and I really am desperate to hear what Cass told Leena.

"Fuck. Fine!" I take a long gulp of my beer. "The night with Cass was... incredible. I wanted to see her again, but she dipped out before I woke up. There's still this crazy connection between us, even though she's trying to act like it's not there. I'm not sure whether I should just give up or push harder. She feels it, but I don't know, man. I can only take so much rejection here."

Bailey nods, processing my confession. "I wouldn't give up yet. She's clearly still thinking about it, based on the conversation she had with Leena earlier this week. Leens thinks Cass is freaked out because she doesn't do relationships, and something about you is different for her. Cass is the definition of a closed book. I know almost nothing about her, and what little I do came from Leena, not Cass."

"That tracks. She wouldn't even tell me her name the night we met."

Bailey nods, clearly already knowing this information. "So, maybe keep trying? If she shuts you down for real, obviously back off. You don't want to get into stalker territory here. She's just got a lot of walls up you may have to break through."

I run a frustrated hand through my hair as I take in his words. It all makes sense. I think she's got layers and layers of barriers to keep other people out. I *know* I broke through some of them during our night together, but I don't want to hurt her by trying to tear down more of them.

I have to take my time on this. It's too important to rush in and risk fucking everything up. Deep in my soul, something is telling me Cass is worth the wait.

A few weeks later, we're all back at the Songbird for the weirdest baby shower I've ever been to, but it's what Jessie and Dan wanted. It's like an open mic night, but it started on Sunday afternoon, there are baby decorations everywhere, and the bar is closed to outside customers.

Mellie was pissed when she couldn't come, but I know the second I let her bail on any amount of Nessa's weekends, it will open the floodgates. In the four months since we moved to Fort Starling, her attitude has only gotten worse. I'm hoping school will help. They started back last week. But I'm honestly concerned about the anger coming from my tiny daughter. If things don't get better, we'll need to get her into some form of therapy. We probably should anyway.

I'm sitting at the bar, watching Dan and Jessie standing together. They're so happy, it makes something in my gut clench to watch them. Being on the brink of divorce is something I wouldn't wish on anyone, and I'm glad they could work it out, but I can't help the brief pang of jealousy. Their family gets to be whole; one unit living together.

Divorcing was the right call for Nessa and me. She was right, as usual. She's my best friend and an amazing mother to my children, but if there was ever a spark of passion between us, it died out a long time ago.

Nessa knew it before I did, and I fought her on it, reluctant to shake up our family for something trivial like passion. But now that I've experienced what a real spark is like, I realize how much was missing from my marriage. I make a mental note to thank Nessa sometime for seeing what I was blind to.

Cass has been floating around the shower, filling drinks. Every so often, Leena or Jessie will make her laugh, and fuck, it reverberates in my chest. It's like my entire being is pulled toward her. When I see her step into the entryway to the kitchen, I decide enough is enough. I follow right behind her, cornering her inside the kitchen entrance.

"Cass, can we talk?"

"What are you doing back here, Griffin?" she asks, clearly annoyed I followed her, but I'm getting desperate. She steps further into the kitchen so we're out of sight of the party.

"Are we ever going to talk about it?" I ask sharply.

"There's nothing to fucking talk about," she lies, panic flickering in her fiery gaze. Her eyes dodge to the side, looking for an escape, but I've got her caged in.

"I can't stop thinking about you... about that night."

"It was one night. You have to let it go."

"Spitfire, please..." I take another step closer to her, as close as I can get without actually touching her. Her breath hitches and speeds up as I move in close.

"Don't call me that!" She pushes at my chest, and I let her move me back a couple of inches, but she keeps her hand on me. There's heat in her eyes, indecision of whether she wants to push me away more or pull me closer. The atmosphere around us thickens.

"Tell me you don't feel this pull. Tell me you don't want me as badly as I want you. Tell me you're not soaking wet for me right now, and I'll drop it."

Our gazes hold, and the spark between us bursts into flames, sending heat through my veins. My dick hardens in my jeans the longer we hold eye contact. Her eyes travel over my face, focusing on my lips. Fuck, I want to kiss her. I want to devour her. But she has to make the first move. She has to give in. Just as I think she's about to cave, she pushes me back again, and I'm startled enough to take a full step back.

"None of that matters. I don't do relationships, Griffin. I don't do complications. And you, Mr. My-boss-slash-best friend's-fiancée's-brother-with-two-kids-and-an-ex-wife, are a walking complication. I'm sorry." Her tone has turned soft and kind, like she's trying to let me down gently, but it's more like she punched me in the gut. She shoots me a sad look and pushes past me to walk back out to the bar.

I preferred her angry insistence that we pretend nothing had happened. This is a whole different thing. She's not denying the chemistry between us. Cass all but admitted she feels the same pull. She just doesn't think it's worth it to see if it could be something real. She sees my kids—the actual loves of my life—as baggage. Fuck, if it doesn't sting.

I run both hands down my face, trying to scrub away the hurt and frustration. I adjust myself to hide the erection I'm still sporting. My feelings are hurt, but I'm still turned on as fuck from being so close to Cass. I take one last deep breath and rejoin the party, grabbing a beer from the bucket of ice they have set up. I down half the beer and plant myself on a couch to stew in my feelings.

I don't stew for long before my phone buzzes, Nessa's name scrolling across the screen. I step out the front door of the bar to take the call.

"Hey Ness, are you guys already at the house? Shit, I lost track of time. I'll be the—"

"We're still on our way," Nessa cuts in quickly, and I blow out a breath of relief. "But Mellie is saying I'm supposed to drop them at the Songbird for a baby shower? Did I miss a memo?"

"No. I told Mellie I'd be home from the party by the time you guys got there."

"Please, Daddy! I want to go to Aunt Leena's Café!" Mellie whines over the speaker.

I sigh. "Low blow, pulling out the 'please Daddy,' Mells. Fine, but only because you don't have school tomorrow. If it's good with you, Nessa?"

"Works for me! I've been dying to meet all of Bailey's crew, anyway! We'll see you in like fifteen."

We disconnect the call, and I pinch the bridge of my nose. I'm already in a sour mood after Cass shot any hope I had to hell. Now, let's add my ex-wife, our angry teenager, and our rambunctious nine-year-old to the party.

Shit. Cass was right. I am a walking complication.

Chapter Six

Cass

I'VE BEEN WATCHING THE door Griffin just disappeared through for ten minutes. Did he leave? Is he okay? His expression when I shot him down is already haunting me, and my stomach is full of knots. *Fuck.* What did I do? I can't help but wonder if I made a big mistake.

As I'm about to go search for him, the door opens and Griffin walks back in. A gorgeous blonde woman trails behind him with two kids who are clearly theirs. The appearance of Griffin's family solidifies every decision I made. I pour myself another drink and sit on a bar stool to sulk, counting down the minutes until this party is over. I could go hide upstairs in my apartment. I doubt anyone would miss me down here.

"Cass!" Leena yells from down the bar. I raise my eyebrows at her. "You're up!"

Right, Jessie wanted this weird-ass baby shower to be an open mic. I make my way up to the stage, doing my best to ignore Griffin and his family sitting at a table in the center of the bar.

I pull the microphone up from where Leena had it on her keyboard. She, of course, sang a slow and lovely melody about motherhood in honor of Jessie and Dan's new arrival. I'm going in a different direction.

"Jessie, it will come as no surprise, I will not be singing about the preciousness of motherhood. Please enjoy my attempt at channeling both Kathy Bates and Carol Burnett. Don't ask me to babysit."

Jessie is laughing, snuggled on a couch with Dan, and I shoot them a wink as the intro music for "Little Girls" from *Annie* plays. Jessie recognizes it almost immediately and laughs harder, holding a hand to her round belly.

I let myself get really into the song. I may be a big fan of resting bitch face most of the time, but musical theater has always been one of my favorite things. It's part of what bonded Leena and me in college.

When I get to the end of the song, I shoot Jessie another wink and take an elaborate bow to Leena and Annie's clapping and heckling. Still smiling and coasting on the adrenaline from performing, I head back to the bar to check on everything.

"*Annie* was my favorite movie for a solid chunk of my childhood. You were awesome," I hear a sweet voice say behind me. "I'm Nessa," the woman says, hand extended to shake mine.

I freeze for just a second before shaking her hand.

"I'm Cass. What can I get you?"

"Can you do an amaretto sour? Some places don't keep amaretto on hand."

I scoff. "You don't know Leena and Annie well, huh? They love their sweet drinks."

"Oh, good. I'll fit right in," she says in a chipper voice. It makes my stomach clench with jealousy. She will fit in perfectly with my friends.

Probably better than I do. She's the opposite of me in almost every way, and it makes me want to hate her, but she seems too nice to hate.

She and Griffin are divorced, but they must get along well if she's here hanging out. This is the type of woman he planned on spending his life with. What the hell was he doing with me?

"Oh, good, Nessa, you've met Cass," Leena says, coming up beside Nessa. She shoots me a questioning expression, and I give her a nod. We're good here. "Cass, did you know Nessa just started a job with Girls on the Run?"

"What? They're my favorite nonprofit! Anytime I do any donating, that's where it goes!" It takes a lot for me to be animated, but talking about the program that tried its best to counteract some of my mother's toxic ideas will do it.

"Amazing! Have you coached? I'm hoping to get some teams going in Fort Starling."

"I haven't coached, but I was actually in the program through my school as a kid in West Virginia. It really helped me."

Nessa's eyes go wide. "Ohmigod! I haven't met many adult women who were GOTR girls! I'd love to come chat sometime and get your opinion on some program things from an alumni perspective."

"Sure." I clam up as I see Griffin walk up to the bar, eyeing the way Nessa and I are chatting. I glance up at him, but he refuses to meet my eye, and the guilt from earlier comes flooding back.

"Griff, Cass was in Girls on the Run as a kid!"

"Very cool," Griffin says politely with a tight smile.

"I'm gonna come hang out and pick her brain sometime." Nessa beams a smile at me, and Griffin winces. He clearly doesn't want his hookup hanging out with his ex-wife. Dammit. This whole thing is fucking awkward.

"Aunt Leena, this place is so cool. I want to come here all the time!" Griffin and Nessa's daughter bounces over to our group.

"You're welcome anytime, Mellie," Leena says warmly. It's a bit strange to see her in family mode. She used to be just as grumpy and deadpan as I am, but she's softened over the last couple of years since Bailey's been in the picture.

"Why don't I come here after school?" Mellie asks. "You guys said I had to find an activity. It could be like an internship."

Griffin and Nessa share a loaded look. "Mells, we meant an activity at school, with other kids."

"I don't want to hang out with other kids. They're cringe. I can hang out here with Aunt Leena and Cass." She turns her pleading gaze on Leena and me. "Aunt Leena, please. I can help however you need. Please save me from a boring club at school."

"Oh, Mellie, I'd say yes, but I'm not actually here all the time. I'm more hands-off these days, and Cass runs the place most of the time."

Shit.

Mellie turns her big, hazel eyes at me, a begging expression all over her pretty little face. I shoot a panicked glance at Griffin and find him smirking at me. Asshole.

"You don't even know me, kid. I could be really mean and terrible to work for. My Miss Hannigan vibes could carry over into real life."

She rolls her eyes with a level of disdain only a teenage girl can manage. "First of all, Aunt Leena likes and trusts you, and I can probably trust her judgment. She wouldn't let you run her business if you were sus. Second, you seem badass with your tattoos, but I can tell at least two of them are *Wicked* themed. Third, I don't think you're as tough as you act; you probably just have unresolved trauma and are all closed off. Fourth, I can handle anything you could dish out."

My eyebrows shoot up, and my jaw drops open. Leena makes a choking sound in the back of her throat, and Griffin covers his mouth to cover the laughter sneaking out of him.

"Wow, are you sure you don't want to join a debate team? Some kind of junior psychologist program?" I ask sarcastically. I have never been so quickly and accurately analyzed in my life. It's like this tiny girl saw to the bottom of my soul and rolled her eyes at what she found. She honestly reminds me so much of myself at her age, and it makes me want to watch out for her. Protect her the way I needed someone to protect me.

Fuck. Fuck. Fuck.

"This is all up to your parents," I say, holding my hands up in surrender. Hopefully, Griffin and Nessa will see how insane this plan would be. Why would they trust me to hang out with their kid? I am not the babysitting type.

Griffin finally comes to the rescue, saying, "Your mom and I will have to discuss it, Mellie."

The girl rolls her eyes again, and her whole body slumps. "Great." She stomps over to where her brother sits and buries her nose in her phone.

Nessa huffs a laugh at her daughter's attitude and shakes her head. "It's like looking in a tiny, mean mirror." She turns back to Leena and me. "Her attitude is my karma for my own teenage years."

"I went through a similar phase," Leena chimes in.

"Same." I take a sip of my drink, nodding, remembering the battles my mom and I had. The big difference here seems to be that these ladies had mothers, or grandmas in Leena's case, who actually loved them.

Griffin laughs. "Why does it feel like I'm being punished then?" His eyes finally find mine, and the intensity from before has returned. "We'll tell her to find something at school. I do not expect you to entertain my kid here."

Our eyes lock for a long moment, heat and longing building between us. I'm about to do something epically stupid, but I can't seem to stop it.

"It would be fine. I mean, she'll probably get bored and hate it here after like a week, anyway."

"This is the most animated I've seen her since we moved, Griff," Nessa chimes in. "If Cass really doesn't mind, we could try it?"

Leena's eyes meet mine for a moment, shooting me a wide-eyed look like she's asking what the fuck I'm doing. If only I knew.

"It's cool with me," I say with fake nonchalance. Inside, I'm panicking, but there's something about Mellie that makes me want to help her.

Griffin studies me, and I give him a shrug. Finally, he nods. "If you're sure, we could try it out this week? The middle school is right down the street, so she could walk over instead of taking the bus home. But only if you're really sure, Spitfire."

My eyes shoot wide at his slip of the nickname. Nessa's head snaps to Griffin, studying the interaction between us in a new light. She might call all this off right now. She stays quiet, but her gaze on me has changed. Intensified. Griffin's definitely gonna have some questions to answer later, but it seems like a him problem.

"I'm fine with it if you're good with it," I say to both Griffin and Nessa. "It's not a big deal."

They share a long look, clearly having one of those telepathic conversations couples who have been together for a long time can have. It makes another punch of jealousy turn my stomach. What the fuck?

"Alright, let's try it," Griffin says. "But if she's in the way or it's a problem, you have to let us know."

I nod my agreement even though I know I'd have Mellie's back even if she gets in my way.

"We're pretty dead here in the after-school hours, so I don't think it'll be an issue."

We agree that Mellie will come to the Songbird after school, starting on Tuesday, since she's off for Labor Day. I get both of their phone numbers to call if there are issues, and they each program mine into their phones and start a group thread between the three of us.

Nessa slides her phone into her purse. "Cass, thank you for this, seriously." She gives me a bright, grateful smile and squeezes my hand. Dammit, I really wanted to hate her when she rolled in here, but I don't think I can. "Griff, I'm gonna say bye to the kids and head out."

"Okay, Ness. Drive safe going home." She pats his shoulder and walks back over to where Mellie and Drew are sitting. Drew gives her a big hug, but Mellie gives her a half-assed pat when Nessa tries to hug her.

Yikes.

"Looks like I've got your name *and* number now, Spitfire," Griffin murmurs so only I can hear him.

I turn my head to look at him, Mellie and her mommy issues forgotten for the moment. The challenge is back in his eyes, and I should be annoyed, but I'm relieved to see it. I was not a fan of the hurt that lingered after our encounter in the kitchen.

"Yeah, well, it's all you're gonna get," I snark at him with an eye roll. I lower my voice more to whisper, "It's called a one-night stand for a reason. One night."

He hums in response and studies my face. I do my best to keep my expression blank, but I can feel the creep of a blush moving across my cheeks. I swallow hard, and he chuckles.

"We'll see, Spitfire. We'll see."

With that, he turns and walks away. He gathers up his children, saying goodbye to Leena, Bailey, and the expectant couple who are snuggled up on a couch. He shoots me a wink right as he walks out the door, and heat floods my body again.

I meant it before; I don't do complications. I don't do more than one night. I don't get attached. These rules have kept me out of messy situations. Kept me from being trapped under someone else's control. Kept me safe.

So why does Griffin make me want to break every single one?

I WAKE EARLY THE next morning to my phone buzzing. I jolt out of bed to grab the phone, sure I'm gonna find my morning barista, Cathy, texting me she can't make it in to open Songbird. Instead, I find a string of messages from Griffin.

Griffin:

> Hey, so I hope you don't feel like we pushed you into something you don't really want to do?

> With Mellie coming to the Café.

> 'Cuz we kinda ambushed you, and I know it's hard to say no to a bunch of people standing in front of you.

> Especially Mellie. I'm still kind of shocked she never ended up with a pony growing up.

> If you don't want Mellie to come, seriously, tell me, and we'll find another activity for her.

> No pressure.

> I'm sorry for texting so many times in a row. I didn't get much sleep.

I laugh to myself at his very clear early-morning spiral. Affection for this man warms my chest, and I shake my head to clear it. I don't do affection, but my guards are down in my sleepy state.

Me:

You done?

Griffin:

Yes. Wait, no.

Good morning, Spitfire.

I groan into my empty apartment as butterflies fill my stomach. Why does Griffin affect me like this?

Me:

I'm fine with Mellie coming to Songbird. I wouldn't have agreed to it if I weren't cool with it. If you haven't noticed, I have no problem letting people know what I think.

Griffin:

Lol, true. I just didn't want to put you in an awkward position.

Me:

Nah, it's cool. I like Mellie. I see a lot of my teenage self in her, so maybe I can help her. I get the feeling she needs someone to talk to.

My phone is still for a minute as the bubbles to show he's typing appear and disappear a few times. Suddenly, it buzzes with an incoming call from Griffin. What the fuck? What kind of psychopath calls someone during a text conversation? I consider declining the call, but answer at the last second instead.

"Are you seriously calling me right now? I almost declined the call and sent you the meme from *The Office* of Kelly telling Jim he can't call someone who texted."

Griffin's laugh is soft and sleepy, making the butterflies take flight again.

Goddammit.

"Sorry, Spitfire, if we're talking about my kid like this, I need to hear your voice. What do you mean you think she needs someone to talk to?"

"I just... I don't know how to explain it. Something in her eyes. I see myself at her age and if..." I take a big breath before letting the truth out. "If I had just one safe adult to talk to at her age, I might not have gone through a lot of what I did."

Griffin's silent for too long, and it makes my anxiety pick up. I want to erase the last minute. Sharing so much, even in the vaguest of terms, makes me antsy.

"I'm not saying you and Nessa aren't safe adults. Divorce is hard on kids, and she may not want to talk to you about it. I don't think anyone's hurting her or she's hurting herself... I'm sorry if I'm overstepping based on a weird gut feeling."

Griffin clears his throat. "Cass?"

"Yeah?"

"I'm sorry you didn't have someone you could talk to. Whatever you've been through. I'm sorry your parents weren't able to protect you."

His words hit like a punch to the gut. I've never talked about my teenage years with anyone other than my therapist. Even Meg and Zander only know about the bare bones of what it was like in my house growing up. Griffin's genuine words are breaking through the armor I've worked so hard to keep strong. I clear my throat, trying to work through the lump in my throat.

"Yeah, well, it's fine. I'm fine."

"Are you, though?" There's a beat of silence before he continues, "Thank you for looking out for Mellie. You'll let me know if there's something serious happening, right? We're already getting on a therapist's schedule, but if there's something urgent, you'll loop us in, yeah?"

"Definitely. I promise."

"Thanks, Cass."

"No problem, buddy." I cringe and cover my face after the nickname leaves my mouth. What the fuck?

"Buddy?"

"Yeah, uh, Slick doesn't really fit you. Especially with the beard."

"Hmm. I don't think you need a new nickname. Spitfire fits you perfectly."

"Well, apparently you're better at nicknames than I am," I say with a laugh.

"Or maybe I'm good at reading you," he replies in a growly voice, and a coil of heat hits my belly that has me squeezing my legs together.

He breaks the spell by asking, "But wait, why 'Buddy'? Like Buddy the Elf or the basketball-playing dog?"

I groan, regretting this phone call deeply. "No, like, we're buddies now, you know." I clear my throat. "Anyway, I'm tired. I'm going back to bed."

"Thanks for the invite, but I've got the kids," Griffin says into the phone, voice low and dangerous.

I bark out a laugh. "I didn't invite you."

"Not yet, Spitfire."

"In your dreams, buddy."

"Always. And Cass? There's not a chance I'll ever think of you as a buddy. Not when I can still vividly remember what it sounds like when you come."

I murmur a panicked goodbye, and I hang up the phone as a shiver runs down my spine, picturing Griffin in my bed.

Fuck.

I'm in trouble here.

Chapter Seven

Griffin

"CASS IS SO FREAKING cool, Dad," Mellie gushes for the millionth time since she started hanging out with Cass three weeks ago. As if she wasn't already on my mind constantly, now hanging out at Songbird is all Mellie talks about. *"Cass is so cool. Cass this, Cass that."*

It doesn't help that Cass is back to icing me out. I thought we were making progress with the phone conversation we had. I finally had a little more insight into why Cass might be so closed off. Now it feels like we're back at square one.

I sigh and do my best to focus on what Mellie's saying as I drive the kids over to Nessa's house. "We don't have school the Monday after next, do you think Cass would let me come to Songbird for the day?" she asks in a hopeful voice.

"I don't know, Mells. Are you sure you want to be there all day?"

"Yeah. It's way better than being at home."

I clench my jaw and grip the steering wheel harder, trying not to let my frustration show. I should be happy that Mellie has found somewhere she likes to be. We've seen such a change in her in the last few weeks. She was so depressed before, not caring about anything or showing interest in her usual hobbies. Between spending time at the Songbird with Cass and talking with a therapist, the shift has been unbelievable.

"I'll ask her when I see her at open mic tonight, Mellie, but no promises."

"Okay, thanks, Dad."

"You guys excited to hang out with Mom this weekend?"

Drew's head pops up from his Switch, and he gives me a big smile in the rearview mirror. "Yes! She said we can go shopping for Halloween decorations now that it's October."

"Mells?"

She shrugs, looking out the window. "It'll be fun, I guess. Cass said I should be nicer to Mom."

My eyebrows shoot up. "She did?"

"Yeah, she pointed out how even though I'm not happy about the divorce and moving, Mom's still a good mom and not everyone is lucky enough to have decent parents."

"Huh. She said all that?" I ask, brow furrowed.

"Kinda. You know Cass. She didn't say it right out, but she made her point. I think maybe her parents were crappy or something."

I don't get to ask any follow-up questions as we pull into Nessa's driveway. Her front door opens as soon as we roll to a stop, like she was watching for us. She's having a hard time getting used to not seeing the kids during the week.

When we decided to move so she could take the Executive Director position at a good-sized non-profit, we agreed it would be better for the kids to stay with me during the week while she's getting her legs under her at the new job. She's the head of the entire organization and has been working crazy hours. When things settle down for her, we'll transition to a more even split.

"My babies!" Nessa yells from her porch. Drew chuckles, and Mellie rolls her eyes, but I can see the smirk she's trying to hide. She gives them both big hugs as they move past her into the house to drop their stuff.

"Hey, you're not gonna say bye?" I call after them. Drew runs full force into me and squeezes me in a hug before running back inside.

"Bye, Dad!"

Mellie gives me a half-assed hug. "Bye, Daddy, don't forget to ask Cass about next Monday!"

"I won't," I say as I kiss the top of her blonde head. Once both kids are inside, Nessa turns to me.

"Ask Cass what about Monday?"

"She wants to hang out at the Songbird on the teacher workday they have coming up. I told her I needed to ask Cass about it."

"It seems to be going well, right?"

"Yeah, Mellie loves it. Cass is harder to read, but I think she'd tell us if it wasn't working."

"So, you and Cass, huh?" Nessa asks with a waggle of her eyebrows. "Am I allowed to ask about your love life, or is it still too soon?"

I bark out a laugh. "Nessa, we've been divorced for over a year, and we were separated for another year before. I think we're fine. It's weird, but fine."

She chuckles. "It is a little weird, but it's part of why we're divorced. So we could both have love lives instead of the celibate roommate thing we had going."

I shake my head at her. "There's not really any love life to discuss with Cass. We, uh... *met* before we had fully moved here while I was in Columbus to complete my job paperwork. It was one night, and she snuck out before I woke up in the morning. I thought I'd never see her again until I walked into Leena's bar."

"You guys haven't been hooking up?" Nessa asks, curiosity glowing on her face.

I roll my eyes at her eagerness and shove my hands in my jeans pockets. "Nope. She called me a walking complication. She said she only does one-night stands."

"Yikes."

"Yeah. There's... I hope this doesn't offend you, but there's a chemistry between Cass and me I've never felt before."

Nessa gives me a sad smile and squeezes my arm. "I'm not offended, Griff. I'm validated. I take it you believe me now when I say something was missing between us? We loved each other, but we never had that spark."

I sigh and tip my head back to look at the sky. "Yes, Nessa. As usual, you were right."

She laughs at my antics. "Music to my ears! So, what's the plan? You gonna win her over?"

"I've tried, but she's so closed off. It's like she puts extra guards up as soon as she sees me coming. Even Mellie knows more about Cass than I do. It's infuriating."

"Oh, you've got it bad. Hang in there, Griff. If she's smart, she'll see what a great guy you are."

"Thanks, Ness. Have a good weekend," I say as I pull Nessa into a friendly hug.

"You too, Griff. Go have fun with your girl."

I bark a laugh as I'm walking back to my car. Fun with my girl? More like an intensely frustrating evening with a woman who won't give me the time of day. Somehow, I'd still choose that with Cass rather than a fun night with anyone else.

I SPOKE TOO SOON. I've been at the Songbird for almost an hour, and other than asking for my drink order in an infuriatingly polite voice, Cass has been ignoring me. It's torture watching her move along the bar, movements fluid. She's wearing her usual uniform, a black V-neck t-shirt and jeans, but tonight she's curled her hair and is wearing a little more makeup. She's fucking stunning.

Her laugh floats down the bar, and I look up sharply to see her chatting closely with a tall, muscular guy. I think he's with one of the bar's beer distributors, judging by the logo on the polo he's wearing. As a straight man, I can admit he's objectively a good-looking dude.

Honestly, he looks a lot like I did the first night I met Cass. He's put together. Clean cut.

Slick.

Fuck. Is he her type?

I glance down at the jeans and casual Henley I'm wearing. My hair's styled to look messy, and I've let my full beard grow in. Maybe she only liked me the night we met because I looked smooth and clean-cut. Now that I've dropped the "meeting your bosses for the first time" style, she's not interested.

With the way she's leaning into this guy and smiling, she's clearly charmed by him. Jealousy races through my veins, insecurity hot on its trail. When she reaches out and squeezes his forearm, her head thrown back in laughter, I snap.

"Hey, Cass," I call out to get her attention. She motions to the guy to tell him she'll be right back.

"What's up?"

"I wanted to chat about Mellie…" I trail off, not sure where I'm even going. I just wanted her to stop talking to this douchebag.

"Oh, sure. Let me finish up with David. I'll be back over in a few." She shoots me a polite smile and goes back over to him.

They're looking over some kind of paperwork, but the smiles and talking in low voices continue. I clench my jaw, my hands tightening into fists.

I know I don't have any claim to Cass. She's made it clear. But the blatant flirting right in front of me wears on my self-control. The jealousy consuming me is taking over the rational side of my brain. Taking control and making me stupid.

They both pull out their phones, clearly making plans to see each other. He finally gathers his shit, kisses her on the cheek, and makes his way out the door. She smiles for a moment after him and then turns to me; her smile falling just enough for my vision to go red with rage.

"Sorry about that."

"Oh, by all means. I just wanted to talk to you about my kid. Why would you cut short setting up your next one-night stand? I hope he knows you only do hookups." I regret saying it immediately, self-loathing making my stomach turn. Cass's head snaps back as if I'd slapped her. I don't miss the flash of hurt crossing her expression before it fills with rage. "Cass, I—"

"Are you fucking kidding me right now?"

"I—"

"No. You don't speak. You listen. How dare you come into my place of work and have the fucking audacity to slut-shame me?" She glares at me. If looks could kill, I'd be on my way to the morgue.

I keep my mouth shut, but put the most apologetic expression on my face I can muster.

"First. What a shitty thing to say to me. You're butthurt I don't want to jump back into bed with you, so you're gonna judge my choices? You didn't seem to have any problem with one-night stands when you were the one fucking me." Her face is turning red, and there's a sheen of unshed tears in her eyes. "Second. It's not even a little bit your business if I want to sleep with someone. Anyone. You don't own me, Griffin."

She grips the edge of the bar, visibly holding herself back. She could probably kick my ass with how angry she is right now. I'd deserve it.

"Finally, not that it concerns you, but David was inviting me to the Halloween party he and his *husband,* Jason, throw every year. He's happily married, and I'm not even close to his type. So, fuck you and your bullshit assumptions, Griffin." She storms away, through the door to the kitchen area. Seconds later, the door to her apartment slams so loud, it echoes through the bar area.

I blow out a big breath and glance around the room. I was here early enough that the bar's not packed yet, but it's not empty either. I'm met with curious glances from the other patrons, so I hunch myself over my phone and ignore them.

I pull up the text thread with Cass, reading through our last messages. Most of them are me trying to start a conversation, and her shutting it down with single-word responses. I type out a long apology, only to delete it immediately. I need to apologize in person. Texting feels like a cop-out.

Relief floods me when I see Bailey and Leena come in the front door. Bailey nods toward an empty table and heads in that direction with the takeout they brought. Leena comes over and hugs me.

"Hi, Griffin, how's it going?"

"Could be better," I grit out.

She looks up at me with a quizzical expression.

"I said something shitty to Cass. She stormed away before I could apologize. She might murder me later."

Leena huffs a laugh. "You'll never see it coming."

"That does not make me feel better, Leens."

She pats my arm and gives me a smile that's more devious than friendly. "It wasn't supposed to. I'll hear her side before I decide whether I'm talking her down or helping her hide your body." She practically skips as she makes her way behind the bar, heading toward Cass's apartment.

I groan and trudge over to the table where Bailey is unloading the Chinese food.

"Hi, big brother! Here's your General Tso's Beef." He hands me the container and then looks up at my face. "What's wrong with you?"

"I fucked up." His eyebrows rise, and he nods for me to continue. "I said something awful to Cass. She probably hates me now and will never speak to me again. I think your fiancée just went to find her so they can plot my murder."

"Yikes, well, you might as well eat. Chinese is a good last meal, right?"

I groan again, but I dig into my food. It gives me something to focus on rather than the huge fucking mess I made with Cass. I have to apologize. As soon as I get a chance, I will grovel. Ask for forgiveness and beg her not to punish Mellie for my asshole behavior.

Fuck.

Mellie will never forgive me if she doesn't get to come to the Songbird anymore. She's just starting to act more like herself. I can't be the reason she spirals again.

I have to fix this.

And not just for Mellie. I can't get the image of Cass's eyes filled with hurt and anger out of my head. It'll haunt me forever if I can't earn her forgiveness. She was right. I don't have any right to be acting like a jealous boyfriend. Cass is free to be with anyone she wants.

I just wish she wanted me as badly as I want her.

Chapter Eight

Cass

I ANGRILY YANK ANOTHER tissue out of the box by my bed. I can't believe I'm crying over Griffin being an asshole. *I don't cry.* What is it about him that has me changing everything about how I do things?

There's a knock at the door. I march over and look through the peephole, relieved to find Leena and not a shamefaced Griffin. I pull the door open and wave her in.

"Hey, Griffin said... Are you fucking crying?" She stares at me with wide eyes. "Holy shit. I didn't even know you could cry. I've never seen it before."

I roll my eyes and huff a laugh at her as I dab the tissue under my eyes.

She plops down on the loveseat. "What the fuck did he say?"

"I was chatting with David. You've seen how we have fun flirting. He reminds me of Zander. Well, Griffin got jealous and said some really slut-shamey stuff about one-night stands."

"Oof, Griffin, you idiot. Did he not realize David's gay?"

"He does now. I went off on him, then ran up here." I was going to cry, and I didn't want Griffin to see it, so I got the fuck out of there.

"So, crying?" Leena's eyebrows raise in question.

I roll my eyes at her. "I'm probably PMS-ing or something."

Leena narrows her eyes at me. She studies my face, and I can't meet her gaze. I grab a couple of waters out of my fridge, doing my best to ignore her scrutiny.

"Oh my god. You like him!"

"I do not. Did you not hear everything I said?"

"I heard you. He's a dumbass for talking to you how he did. But I'm focused on your reaction. He's under your skin, and he hurt your feelings."

I scoff. "I don't get my feelings hurt. I'm immune." It's close to the truth. It takes a lot to ruffle my feathers. Years of your own mother saying vile things to you will force you to grow up with a thick skin.

"I think with anyone else, it's true. But Griffin's different."

"I don't want him to be different," I whisper with my eyes clenched tightly shut.

"I know, babes, but he is. And he's not going anywhere anytime soon. He's Bailey's brother. It's not like we can ban him from our friend group just because you want to bone him again but don't want to admit it."

"Are you sure?"

"I'm sure. He definitely thinks we may be plotting his murder, though."

I laugh. "I reamed him out before I came up here. He seemed sorry almost immediately after he realized what he said."

"Oh, he's down there beating himself up. He's pretty sure you hate him now," she says with a laugh.

"I wish I hated him. It would make my life easier."

"I know. I do think you need to make him suffer, though."

I hum in response, drinking my water and trying to think of ways to torture him. A devious thought occurs to me. "This all started because he was jealous. Maybe I should lean into it a bit more before I let him grovel."

"How? Are you gonna go down there and find someone to flirt with?"

"I don't want to give anyone the wrong idea."

"Oh shit... I've got an idea." I gesture for her to continue. A devious smile blooms on her face, and a hint of evil glints in her hazel eyes. "'Bring On the Men.' Do you still remember the song?"

My eyebrows wing up at the mention of the song we used to sing all the time in college. "I'd probably need to take a glance at the lyrics, but yeah, it'll come back to me."

"Okay, let's get Jessie and Annie in here. They can help us with those chorus parts. We'll make sure we all remember it, you'll change into a sluttier outfit, and we'll find some guys in the audience and prep them, make sure they're aware you're trying to make someone else jealous. Griffin won't know what hit him."

"If it's anything like earlier, he'll get mad again. I fucking dare him to act like he owns me again, the asshole."

Leena laughs. "Griffin is a walking green flag. He said something shitty out of jealousy, but he's not a bad guy."

I sigh. "I know. I just... can't do the complicated thing."

Leena hums and studies me again. "Can't do the complicated thing, or are afraid of catching actual feelings?"

Damn her for knowing me too fucking well.

I shrug, and she smirks at me, knowing she's right. I am afraid of catching feelings. I'm fucking terrified. Because what if I decide to let Griffin in and he realizes I'm not cut out for relationships? What if he realizes I'm not worth more effort than a quick one-night stand?

I've never let anyone get close enough to have my biggest fears confirmed. That my mom has been right all along. I'm a waste of space.

Unloveable.

I've never been brave enough to let anyone get to know me well enough to love me. I'm not sure it's possible. But if there was anyone in the world I wanted to give a chance to...

Griffin would be the one.

AFTER RUNNING THROUGH THE song a couple of times to refresh our memories, the girls head down to the bar to get ready while I change my outfit. Instead of my normal black tee and jeans, I change into a sheer black button-down top and a flirty black mini-skirt. The shirt is so see-through, my red lacy bra is visible underneath. There's a line in the song about black and red lace, and I fully intend to flash my bra at the crowd.

I refresh the makeup that got all smudged during my freak crying jag and add a deep red lip. I study myself in the mirror for a long moment. I look sexy, but I can still see the sadness lingering in my eyes. Gotta get rid of that before I go out there.

I refuse to show any hint of weakness. I can't afford for Griffin to get all sensitive and nice on me. I want him mad and jealous. He's easier to resist this way.

When I pop out into the bar, I scan the room, doing my best to avoid Griffin's gaze. I can feel his eyes on me as he takes in my wardrobe change, and it's all I can do to keep my eyes on Leena talking to a group of young guys who are sitting at the front near the tiny stage. She meets my eyes and gives me a small nod, confirming she's filled the guys in on what's about to go down.

On the other side of the room, Dan and Jessie are talking with their heads close together. They look a little like they're arguing, but Jessie still has a big smile on her face despite Dan's frown. He reaches out to run his hand along her massive baby bump, and his expression softens. She pushes up to kiss him, and he shakes his head and moves to sit at the table where Griffin is sitting with Bailey and Eric.

The girls congregate back at the bar with me, and I pour us a round of drinks, Sprite for Jessie, of course. I need a little liquid courage before we get into the performance.

"Okay, the guys up front are in. Except for the one in the red shirt, he's engaged and doesn't want to cause problems."

I eye the group, mapping out my plan. "I'll probably aim for the one in the black shirt up front anyway, this way I can still be mostly facing the crowd. Will you warn him I'm probably going to sit on his lap, Leens? Maybe let him grab my ass on that buns line?"

"On it!" Leena bounces over to the guys. I shake my head at how excited she is about helping me get revenge on her almost brother-in-law. I turn my eyes to Jessie and Annie to find similar glee on their faces.

"Y'all are way too excited about this plan," I grumble through my nerves. I perform at open mics all the time without getting nervous, but this one hits different and makes my stomach clench. Annie and Jessie chuckle at me.

"Making a man jealous after he said something shitty? I'm here for it." Annie shrugs as she sips on her amaretto sour.

"Plus, we both had our own drama in the past year. It's fun to be on this side of things," Jessie chimes in.

"Facts."

I shake my head at their antics. I sneak a glance at Griffin to find him still staring at me, brow furrowed as Dan talks. I can tell from here that he wants to come over and talk to me, but the guys are keeping him at the table. Butterflies flutter in my stomach when our eyes meet, and I do my best to keep my expression angry. *Fucking butterflies?* What the fuck is happening to me?

"Dan is debriefing the guys," Jessie pulls my attention back from Griffin's longing gaze. "Leena said we'll wait a bit before we do the song, let the open mic get rolling."

I nod. "Okay. I'll help Alaina with the bar until I get the signal."

"He's not gonna know what hit him, Cass. You're fucking hot."

I chuckle and shake my head at my friends, marveling at how much closer we've all gotten over the last couple of years. Not long ago, I would have thought of them as Leena's friends. I'm not sure exactly when things shifted, but I'm happy to have these women in my corner.

They send winks my way as they take their drinks to a table near the front, where they're hanging out until it's time for our song. I take a big breath to steel myself, risking one more glance at Griffin. His eyes are on Dan this time, arms crossed and a deep frown on his face. He's clearly being warned about what's coming and does not seem happy.

Good. Let him get angry. His coming at me all possessive is exactly what I need to remind me why I don't do complications. With that thought in mind, I put my head down and focus on tending bar, ready for what comes next.

Chapter Nine

Griffin

WHEN LEENA REAPPEARS IN the bar after being in Cass's apartment for half an hour, she shoots me an evil smile and makes a beeline for a group of guys at the front of the room. I glance at Bailey, who is watching her curiously but doesn't seem concerned.

"I think the girls are up to something," I murmur to him.

"They definitely are, but I don't know what it is yet."

Annie and Jessie appear from the kitchen area next, laughing and sharing devious smiles. The two of them have a quick conversation with their other halves. Eric shakes his head and heads our way, while Dan and Jessie talk longer.

"Somebody's in trouble," Eric singsongs as he sits down at our table, confirming the girls are out for revenge.

I groan and run a hand through my hair, and Cass makes her way out from the kitchen doorway. She's changed clothes and put on heavier makeup. I swallow hard and shift in my seat. I take a deep breath, willing the tightness in my jeans at her appearance to go down.

Before I can ask Eric what's going on, Dan stomps his way over to us.

"What did you do?" he asks gruffly, and he plops into his chair.

I sigh. "I fucked up with Cass earlier. I said something really shitty out of jealousy, and I'm pretty sure she hates me now."

"She's definitely pissed, but I doubt she hates you. I don't think they'd all be plotting to make you more jealous if she wanted nothing to do with you."

My eyebrows shoot up. "What do you mean?"

"You ever hear the song 'Bring on the Men' from the *Jekyll & Hyde* musical?" Dan asks.

Bailey and I both shake our heads.

Eric huffs out a laugh, taking a drink of his beer before Dan continues, "They all got obsessed with the musical in college. I think it was Jessie's junior year, so Cass's freshman year. They teamed up to learn the song and like to bring it out every so often when they're feeling fiery. I'm pretty sure in the show, the song is set in a brothel, if that gives you any idea of where they're going with this."

"I saw them do it once a few years ago when Annie still hated me," Eric mumbles. "It's hot, and they're definitely trying to torture you for getting jealous earlier."

I run a hand over my face and cross my arms over my chest. Part of me wants to be annoyed that the girls are plotting instead of just letting me apologize to Cass. But the other part can't quite tamp down the hope this means Cass feels more for me than she's been willing to admit.

"Here's how it's gonna go. When Leena gives the signal, Eric and I have been instructed to move to the sides of the room so our girls can spread out in the room. Bailey, you're on Griffin babysitting duty because Leena will be at the keyboard. Make sure he doesn't start a fight with those pretty boys up front or interrupt the song."

"I'm not gon—"

"Like I said. Stay in your seat, wait it out, then maybe Cass will let you apologize," Dan says sternly. "And if you want some advice, keep your cool when you talk to her. She's looking for a reason to keep you out, and getting all pissed at her will only validate her pushing you away."

I'm taken aback by his advice. "I didn't realize you knew Cass so well."

Dan grins at me. "I don't. That advice came from my wife. She's apparently rooting for you." I huff out a laugh and shake my head, taking a large gulp of my beer.

Bailey laughs, too. "She can't resist matchmaking, can she?" he asks, smiling, warmth in his voice.

"Nope. Even at almost nine months pregnant, she can't stop herself from meddling. Shit. Leena's giving the signal." He and Eric stand to move to their assigned spots in the crowd, and I blow out a big breath.

"This is gonna suck, isn't it?" I ask Bailey in a low voice.

He chuckles and pats me on the shoulder. "Probably. You heard Dan—just keep your cool. She's doing this to rile you up."

Before I can respond, Leena's voice comes over the microphone.

"Hi everyone! We have a real treat for you tonight. Our very own Cass Ortiz is going to sing a little number for you, and I hope you're all ready for her." Leena chuckles low into the microphone, making eye contact with me, and my nerves ratchet up another notch.

When Cass crosses out from behind the bar, my breath freezes in my lungs. I saw her sheer top and red bra, but the bar had blocked my view of the very short skirt she's wearing. I clench my jaw, tension filling my body at the sight of her long tan legs on display. She's paired the skirt with heels, making her legs seem miles long.

Leena plays the vampy song, and Cass sings in a rich alto tone. The lyrics talk about sleeping with as many men as possible, and at one point, she pulls her already sheer shirt off her shoulder to put one side of her red bra on display. The girls join in singing the chorus with her, getting into the spirit of the rowdy song.

I watch her pace the stage with my hands balled into fists. During a music break, she gets off the stage to roam the room with Annie and Jessie. When both of them find Dan and Eric in the crowd, Cass moves toward the table of young guys at the front. They're in their mid-twenties and are all smiling when they see her coming.

The song slows down, and Cass plops herself into one of the guy's laps. She leans in to whisper in the guy's ear, and my earlier jealousy rears its head. She moves to stand between two of the guys when the lyrics are talking about a threesome, and she playfully tussles the hair of the guy whose lap she sat in.

Cass turns her backside to the audience to walk back to the stage on a line that says something about buns, and the dude close to her dares to reach out and grab her ass. I let out a low growl, and Bailey squeezes my shoulder, reminding me to stay in my seat.

Cass doesn't seem mad at the guy who grabbed her, smirking and raising an eyebrow in my direction. It's like she's daring me to react, so I stay where I am as she sings about an orgy or something. By this point, the entire crowd is into the song, with even more people singing along to the obscure number. Only at the Songbird are random Broadway songs the norm.

Finally, after what has seemed like hours, the song is over. Cass is flushed from the performance, and I'm stunned all over again by how fucking gorgeous she is. I know she was trying to make me mad and jealous with this whole performance, and I'll admit, I did not love seeing another man's hand on her, but more, I'm hit by how much I want her. She's incredible, and I need to make sure she knows it.

I stand up, and Bailey meets my eyes. "You good, Griff?"

I nod and pat him on the shoulder. "Yeah. I'm gonna go apologize for earlier."

"Okay, man. Good luck!"

I shoot him a grateful smile as I make my way over to Cass, who is chatting with the guy she let touch her earlier. I must still look pissed off because he tenses when he sees me coming over her shoulder. He leans in to murmur something in her ear before he turns away and heads toward the bar.

Cass straightens her spine and turns to face me, arms crossed. She looks ready for a fight, but I'm not gonna give her one.

I clear my throat. "You were amazing up there," I say sincerely, and her jaw drops in surprise. I smile, happy to have caught her off guard. "Can we talk? Maybe in private?" I give her my most pleading expression, begging her with my eyes to talk to me.

She gives me a tight nod and motions with her head toward the entrance to the kitchen that will lead to her apartment upstairs.

"Let me make sure Leena and Alaina have the bar covered," she mumbles.

I nod, and she moves toward Leena, who's back at the bar with Annie and Jessie. The girls have a tense huddle, looking back at me every so often.

After a few minutes, Cass nods, and Leena pulls her into a hug, whispering something in her ear that makes Cass tense even more. She turns to look at me, her mouth pressed into a hard line, and gestures for me to follow her. We move through the back kitchen area to a set of stairs along the back wall.

I try and fail to keep my eyes off the very short skirt Cass is wearing. I catch a peek of red lace as she takes a step up, and I swallow a groan. She unlocks the door to the apartment and ushers me in.

I scan the small one-room apartment slowly. In the corner to the left of the door, she has a small kitchenette with narrow appliances and a round table with two chairs. The right-side corner has a plush tan loveseat aimed at a medium-sized TV set on top of a generic entertainment center. I look away quickly from the king-size bed sitting in the center of the back wall, a black and purple floral comforter covering the bed.

Cass clears her throat, pulling my focus to her. "You said you wanted to talk. So talk." Her voice is angry, but I've studied her enough these last few months to see the underlying hurt she's trying to hide. She crosses her arms and raises an eyebrow.

"I'm sorry." Both eyebrows go up, but she stays tense with her arms crossed, so I continue, "I should never have said what I said. I was angry and jealous, but it's no excuse for treating you the way I did."

I move a step closer to her, bending slightly so I can look directly into her eyes. I need her to see I mean every word I'm saying. "I'm so incredibly sorry, Cass. You're right. I don't have any claim on you, even though I wish I did." She blows out a shaky breath, but still doesn't respond.

I reach out to grip her upper arms slowly, giving her plenty of time to pull back or stop me. "Our night together... It changed something in me. I didn't know that the chemistry we have between us was a real thing that was possible. I've never experienced it with anyone else, and I let the connection go to my head. I'm sorry for acting like a jealous idiot when I had no right."

She studies my eyes for a long moment, searching them for a lie she won't find. She blows out a big breath, and I can feel the tension release where I'm holding her arms. I'm about to let go of her and step back when she clenches her eyes shut for a second. When they open, I freeze at the heat I find in her gaze.

"Fuck it." With that, she launches herself at me, connecting our lips in a hard kiss. It takes me a second to figure out what the hell is happening, but when I do, I wrap my arms around her, pulling her against my body, eliminating any space between us.

I slant my mouth over hers, devouring the lips I've missed every single second since she left my hotel bed in March. I roam my hands down her back, gripping her skirt in both hands, letting my fingers tease along the underside of her ass cheeks.

Cass moans into my mouth at the contact, and I press my hips forward so she can feel just how much she's affecting me through my jeans.

"Griffin," she pants out my name, and I swear my brain chemistry rearranges at the sound. Over the last couple of months, I've hated the polite way she said my name, missing the sound of the cheeky nickname from our time together. *But this?* Her saying my name like a plea drives me wild.

"What do you need, Spitfire?" I murmur as I kiss my way down her neck, moving her sheer shirt down her shoulder. I press her back against the apartment door.

"I need you. Now. I need you to fuck me right here." Her hands grab at my belt. I grab my wallet out of my pocket to grab the condom I keep there. I toss the wallet to the floor as she pushes my jeans and boxer briefs down. I make quick work of sheathing myself in the latex and move to lift her against the door.

"There's a whole bar full of people down there. You'll have to stay quiet, or everyone will hear me fucking you."

"I don't care," she moans as she threads her fingers into my hair. "I don't care who hears."

"Good. When I'm done, everyone down there will know you're mine." Just when I think I went too far, she lets out a whimper.

"Please... Griffin, please fuck me."

I groan and balance her into the door, holding her with one hand so I can move my other between us. "Shit," I murmur as my hand finds the damp lace barrier between us.

"Just push 'em to the side," Cass whines in my ear.

"Fucking Christ, Cass. You're gonna be the death of me."

Her low chuckles turn into a gasp as I follow her instructions, sliding the wet lace to one side and swiping a finger through her arousal. I vow to take my time with round two to reacquaint myself with every inch of her, but right now, she's begging for me to fuck her. I couldn't deny her even if I wanted to. I line myself up to her entrance and with one hard thrust, I sheath myself fully inside her tight pussy, drawing a groan from both of us.

"Fuck, you're so tight, Spitfire." I pull back and slam home again, her inner walls already fluttering and squeezing.

"Been a while..." she pants in my ear as I find my rhythm. "Hasn't been anyone since you."

I almost come on the spot. I still my thrusts and pull back to gaze into her eyes. They're full of heat and something else, something vulnerable that makes my chest squeeze.

"Same for me. It's only been you." I rest my forehead against hers and start moving again. She cries out as I pump harder, wanting to own her. I want her to feel me when we're done here. "You're mine, Cass. Please tell me you're mine."

"I'm yours. I'm yours, Griffin."

Her words flood my veins with heat, and I capture her lips as I keep driving my hips into her. It only takes a few thrusts before her orgasm takes over, her whole body tensing in my arms. I follow her quickly over the edge with her words ringing in my ears.

She's mine.

Chapter Ten

Cass

I'M YOURS.

The words are still repeating in my head as Griffin and I come down from the crazy against-the-door sex we just had. We're both breathing hard as he carries me over to the bed and gently lays me down.

"Let me get rid of the condom," he murmurs with a kiss to the top of my head. I nod and fling an arm over my face to calm the fuck down. I wait for regret to fill me at what we did, at the words I said in the heat of the moment, but it never comes. I'm stunned to realize I meant it.

Shit. What does this even mean? Does he expect me to be his girlfriend now? What about the kids? I'm not stepmom material.

Fuck.

"Cass?" Griffin's voice is cautious as he lies down next to me on the bed. He gently pulls my arm away from my face, and I glance up at his concerned face. "Are you spiraling?"

"No!" He quirks an eyebrow at me and smirks. "Fine, yes."

He chuckles and tucks a stray chunk of hair behind my ear. "Just tell me what you're thinking."

"For one, I swore we weren't gonna do this. Something about you makes me break all of my own rules." I pause and take a deep breath. "And I don't know how to do this."

"Do what?"

"Relationships. Commitment. Any of it. I've never been in a relationship."

"Never?" he asks, his voice surprised.

"Never, and I know what I said during... but I don't know how to be yours." I cover my face with my hands again. I'm suddenly embarrassed because what kind of thirty-year-old is this freaked out by the idea of a relationship?

"Spitfire, look at me." I pull my hands down to find Griffin smiling softly down at me. "I would never hold you to anything you said in the heat of the moment. This doesn't need to be anything you don't want it to be. If you want us to be done here, I'll find a way to be okay with it."

My stomach flips at his soft words. The idea of him walking away now fills me with fear, and I have my answer. "I don't want us to be done," I whisper, moving my hand to cup his cheek.

His eyes close at the touch, and his body relaxes with relief that I'm not pushing him away again. He brings his hand and places it over mine on his face.

He opens his eyes to meet my gaze. "Then we'll figure it out together. We don't need to put labels or rules on it. We can take it slow."

I nod and study his warm hazel eyes, relaxing knowing he's not going to push me into anything I'm not ready for.

"One thing though... can we..." he trails off, clearly nervous to finish his sentence.

"Can we what?"

He swallows and presses his lips together before answering. "I'd prefer it if we were exclusive. I had no right to act like such a jealous idiot today, but I can't... I can't share you."

I huff a laugh. "Griffin. I haven't slept with anyone since you, back in March. I'm not gonna start now that we're together or whatever."

He blows out a breath and gathers me in his arms as he relaxes into my bed. I let my body relax too, enjoying the feeling of being held, something I never liked before Griffin. We cuddle together in comfortable silence until my stomach growls so loudly we both start laughing.

"Work up an appetite there, Spitfire?" he teases.

"More like I was too focused on revenge to eat dinner," I snark back at him.

He groans and sits up. "Ugh. My stupid, jealous rage ruined your night."

I laugh as I sit up next to him. "I don't know. I had a lot of fun watching you stew in your seat when I flashed the room my bra and let Matt grab my ass."

Griffin lets out a low growl and frowns. "I'm pretty sure I have bruises from Bailey forcing me to stay in my seat when he grabbed you."

I laugh again. "I told him to do it, killer. I figured it would make you crazy after you were ready to murder David earlier."

He rolls his eyes and gives me a sheepish look. "Come on. Let's get you some food. Can't have you teasing me on an empty stomach."

I laugh again and follow him over to my tiny kitchen area. He opens the fridge and makes a tsk-ing sound.

"Cass, why don't you have any food in here?" he asks, voice full of concern.

"I usually do groceries on Saturday afternoons. You caught me right at the end of my supply."

"Let's go, Spitfire. I won't have you going hungry on my watch."

I chuckle as I strip out of the damp, stretched-out lace underwear and replace them with a simple black cotton pair. When I'm situated, I follow Griffin out the door, somehow content to go wherever he leads.

AN HOUR LATER, WE'RE back in my apartment with our haul of assorted fast food. We hit four separate drive-throughs to create a feast of late-night snacks. When I couldn't decide what sounded good, Griffin insisted on getting everything I was craving. I was a little stunned he was willing to go through all the trouble just because my stomach was being picky.

My particular history with disordered eating has left me unable to eat something that doesn't sound good in the moment. It will literally make my stomach turn, and if I try to ignore it, I'll gag on the food. It's part of the reason I only do small batches of grocery shopping, hence the empty fridge.

Griffin spreads all the food out on my tiny kitchen table, while I grab us a couple of plates. "Do you want a beer?" I ask.

"Nah, I'm good with the milkshake," he says. "Although I'm probably gonna have heartburn in the middle of the night."

I snicker. "I forgot about you being an old man. Isn't it past your bedtime?"

He pinches my hip as I pass him to take my seat, laughing at my teasing. "I'm not an old man."

"Isn't forty considered middle age?" I ask in a saccharine voice.

He points a finger at me. "Rude. Now eat your food, Spitfire."

"Yes, sir."

He groans and tips his head back, swearing under his breath.

I chuckle and pop open the lid of cheese sauce to dip my nacho fries. We fall into a companionable silence while we eat. When I've had my fill of grease and salt, something he said earlier tonight comes to mind.

"Did you actually want to talk about Mellie earlier?"

He huffs and shrugs before giving me a sheepish look. "Technically, I was supposed to ask you if she can come hang out at Songbird for the day off she has the Monday after next, but really, I was trying to get you to stop talking to the guy."

I laugh and shake my head. "I can't believe you didn't know David's gay."

"I've seen him around the bar before, but I've never spoken to him," he says with a shrug. "I'm sorry again for reacting the way I did. I got all in my head and insecure."

"Insecure about what?" I ask curiously.

He pulls on the back of his neck, embarrassed to have to explain his behavior, but I don't back off from my question. I want to understand what was going through his head before he said something shitty. I need to know whether this will be a pattern or if it was a one-off. I may not have experience being in a relationship, but I know how it feels to have someone saying vicious things all the time, and I can't deal with it.

"I was watching you flirt with David, and I started to realize he had the same clean-cut vibe I had the night we met. I thought maybe he was your type and..." He blows out a big breath before continuing. "I realized I've let my beard grow in and haven't worn a suit in weeks since I work from home so much. I thought that might be why you weren't interested in me anymore."

The sheer vulnerability in his eyes melts any annoyance I held onto. I stand from my seat and move to his side of the table. He leans back in the chair as I drop myself onto his lap, my legs off to one side. His arms instantly loop around me, and he lowers his head to nuzzle his face into the crook of my neck.

I run my fingers through the short beard on his cheek. "Do you want to hear what I thought when I first saw you in the bar?"

"I'm not sure. Do I?"

I laugh and tell him anyway. "I thought you were too pretty and clean-cut to be my type." He leans back to look at me with his eyebrows raised in question. I shrug and add, "I have a history of going for guys with beards and tattoos. So actually, you're more my type now than you were when we met."

He drops his head onto my shoulder, laughing. "Would have been helpful information earlier today."

I chuckle and run my hands through his hair. "It was never about not wanting you. It was about my being scared of *how much* I wanted you."

He blows out a shaky breath and raises his head from my shoulder. He stares into my eyes, studying me. "So what you're saying is I'm exactly your type, and you've just been denying it for months?" He gives me a cocky smirk, and I roll my eyes, trying to get off his lap, but he bands his arms around me.

"Keep it up, and I'll kick you out of my apartment," I grumble.

He laughs. "No, you won't, Spitfire. At least not until you get some beard burn between those pretty thighs."

My body lights up at his dirty words. I do my best to fight down the shiver that slides down my spine, thinking about his head between my legs. I blow out a big fake sigh. "I guess we can try it. You can stay for now."

Griffin pinches my side, tickling me and making me yelp, before gathering me in his arms and standing. He walks the short distance to my bed and tosses me onto the surface, making me laugh again as I bounce.

My laughter dies in my throat as he grips my ankles and pulls me to the edge of my bed. Thanks to my short skirt, he has easy access to the black cotton underwear I tossed on before we went to get food. He makes quick work of sliding them off and does exactly what he said he would.

It's only later, when I'm drifting off to sleep, wrapped in his strong arms, that I realize he's the first man I've ever let into my bed. I can't help but wonder what other rules I'll break to stay close to this man, and I'm terrified all over again.

Some rules aren't meant to be broken.

"You could've stayed home and slept in, you know!" Mellie's eyes snap open at my words, and she sits up to take a drink of the frozen coffee drink I made her. It's mostly milk and sugar, partially because it's how she likes it, and partially because I have no idea what the rules are with kids and caffeine. I make a mental note to check in with Griffin about it.

"I didn't want to stay home with Drew and my dad!" She rolls her eyes and makes a gagging sound. I chuckle as I make a latte for a customer.

As much as I was worried about spending time with a teenager, I enjoy my days with Mellie. She reminds me so much of myself. Like who I could have been if my childhood hadn't been so fucked up.

"Whatever you say, Mellie!" I tell her with a smile as I hand the customer her drink.

"Amelia."

I stop and study the serious expression on the kid's face. "What?"

She blows out a breath. "I want to be called Amelia."

I nod, thinking her request over. "Okay. Works for me. Just remind me if I forget, yeah?"

Her mouth gapes a bit. "That's it?"

"Well, yeah? Did you think I'd try to talk you out of it? It's your full name, right?"

"Yes, but no one calls me Amelia. Except for the kids and teachers at school, actually. It's how I introduced myself. I figured since I'm the new kid, I can be anyone I want. But my family has never called me anything but Mellie."

"You don't need to convince me. Clearly, I know all about choosing a name that feels more like you."

"What is Cass short for?" she asks, eyes narrowing. "Cassandra?"

"That is classified. There are only a few people who are allowed to use my full name, and I'm not about to spill it to you, my friend."

Mellie—I mean Amelia—gasps. "I can totally keep a secret."

I raise my eyebrows and stare her down. She lifts her chin defiantly, and I chuckle. I hold my hand out, pinkie finger extended toward her. "You swear you can keep this top-secret information to yourself?"

She gives me the standard teenage look of disdain and rolls her eyes hard. "A pinkie promise? Really, Cass? I thought you were cooler than this."

I don't move from my stance, eyebrows raised in challenge.

She sighs before linking her pinkie with mine. "Fine. I won't tell," she huffs with another eye roll.

I chuckle at her antics. "It's Cassidee. Spelled with a double 'e' at the end. As if it already wasn't way too girly of a name, my mother spelled it in a stupid way."

"Oof, yikes. Yeah, it doesn't fit you at all. I like Cass way better."

"You and me both, kid." I study her for a minute, thinking of her name. "Amelia and Mellie both fit you."

She shrugs. "It's not like I don't like Mellie. Amelia feels more grown up, more like who I wanna be for high school next year."

I nod. "Fair. Well, I'll do my best to make the switch. Your parents will probably have a harder time switching because they've known you one way for so long, but I'm sure they will make the change when you explain it's important to you."

"Did your parents switch to calling you Cass?"

I clench my jaw just thinking about my parents and the endless arguments we had on the subject. "My parents aren't a good frame of reference," I grit out.

"What do you mean?" Her wide hazel eyes shine with innocence and remind me so much of Griffin that it steals my breath for a second. This is his little girl. I'd better tread carefully here.

"You know how I keep reminding you that your mom's a pretty good mom and she's trying to do her best for you and your family?"

Amelia rolls her eyes and huffs, "Yeah?"

"I didn't have that. I don't have a good mom. In fact, she was actually a terrible mom. My dad was better, but he still let a lot of stuff happen he shouldn't have."

I'm flooded with memories. Memories of my mother screaming in my face. Memories of slaps and pinches. Memories of backhanded compliments, gaslighting, and actual starvation. And memories of my dad doing nothing. Of him bailing and living his own life when he couldn't handle her shit anymore. Of leaving me to fend for myself.

"Cass!" Amelia yells, and it's pretty clear she said my name a few times.

I blink the tears out of my eyes. *Fuck.*

This is why I do my best not to think about my childhood. I did my time in therapy. I spent years working through everything my first eighteen years put me through. I may not be the most well-adjusted person, but I haven't had a flashback in a long time.

I shake my head and focus back on Amelia's concerned face. "Anyway. Your parents are not like my parents."

She nods but is still watching me like I might do something crazy at any minute.

I clear my throat and bring the conversation back to her. "You still pissed about the divorce? Or are you feeling better about it?"

She lets out another enormous sigh. "Better, I guess. It's hard to be too pissed at them when they seem so much happier." I gesture for her to continue. "I can tell Mom really loves her new job, and she said it won't be too much longer before we can be at her house the same amount of time as Dad's."

She slurps on the straw of her drink, getting all the whipped cream from the bottom of the cup. My curiosity finally gets the better of me. "What about your dad?"

She shrugs. "He was pretty miserable for a while there, but in the last week or so, he's been a lot happier. He was even singing in the shower this morning before I left!" She gives me an appalled expression and shakes her head in disapproval.

I bite the inside of my cheek so hard I taste blood. There's a good chance I'm the reason for his fluctuating moods. I get Amelia started on learning how to make frozen lattes, and I fight to keep a smirk off my face as I think about the stolen moments Griffin and I have had in the last week.

It was his weekend with the kids, but we saw each other last week during lunch breaks and a couple of late-night hookups in my car in his driveway.

Griffin insisted I could come into the house. He'd be fine if the kids knew about us. But what would we even tell them? We still haven't labeled what it is we're doing, and I don't want to confuse them when Griffin inevitably tires of my complete lack of relationship experience.

It's only a matter of time.

Chapter Eleven

Griffin

"MELLIE, YOUR MOM'S ALMOST here!" I shout up the stairs while making sure Drew has all the accessories for his costume in his bag. He's dressing up as Peter Pan for the third year in a row, but this year we upgraded his costume to include tights, shoe covers, and a tiny plastic dagger. Nessa's taking the kids to her office's trunk or treat, so I'm pretty sure she's dressing up as Captain Hook or Tinkerbell. Mellie, of course, refused to take part in their group costume.

"Dad?" Mellie's voice is tentative, causing me to pause my packing and glance up at her standing halfway down the stairs. "I don't want to go with Mom tonight."

I blow out a big breath. "Mellie, I thought we were past all this," I say carefully, not wanting to start a fight.

"No, it's not that I don't want to go, but... a couple of the girls in my English class live a few streets over, and they invited me to walk around and get candy with them tonight."

My eyebrows shoot up. This is the first time Mellie's mentioned making friends at school. "You want to go trick-or-treating?"

Mellie rolls her eyes with a huff. "I guess technically. We're pretty sure this is the last year we can get away with it. They're dressing up as Huntrix and needed a Mira, and I mentioned that I had the costume Grandma sent me. Plus, I still have the pink hair chalk from my birthday."

My sexy Halloween plans with Cass float down the drain as I realize I can't deny Mellie the chance to make real friends here. I was already planning on passing out candy in our neighborhood before heading over to Songbird's Halloween open mic party. Now it looks like I'll be home for the evening.

I sigh and nod. "It's fine, Mell. I'll just text Uncle Bailey and let him know I'm not gonna make it to the Halloween open mic." I pull out my phone to actually text Cass about the change in our plans, but Mellie doesn't need that information.

Mellie gasps dramatically before shrieking, "I could go with you! Oh, please, Daddy! I want to go to an open mic!"

"Mellie, I'm not sure it's really kid-friendly, especially with it being Halloween."

"Text Cass to check! Or Aunt Leena! I swear I can handle it!"

I sigh, thinking it over. I've never seen open mic get too rowdy or too inappropriate, even when I've been there until close, but I'm not sure if the holiday will make a difference. "Fine. I'll ask Cass, but if she says it's not appropriate, we're leaving it there, yeah?"

"Okay! Thank you, Daddy! I'm gonna go finish my hair before Liv and Celeste are ready!"

I shake my head as she pounds up the stairs and open my text thread with Cass.

Me:

I'm sorry to change our plans for the night, but Mellie finally made some friends here, and they want her to go trick-or-treating with them. I can't say no. I'm sorry.

Cass:

It's okay. I'm glad she's finding friends at school.

Me:

She wants to come to open mic. I said I had to check with you whether it's appropriate.

Cass:

Yeah, should be fine. The content of songs may be a little risque, but it shouldn't get too wild, especially not early in the night.

Me:

Okay, cool. So I'll still see you, I'll just have a teenager with me.

Cass:

You should probably be glad she wants to hang out with you instead of getting drunk in a field somewhere with her friends.

Me:

Pretty sure it has more to do with wanting to hang out with YOU. Maybe I can just lock her up and not let her go anywhere for the next five years. It'll work, right?

Cass:

Nope. Then she'll just go crazy as soon as she gets freedom in college and will completely cut off all contact with you.

Me:

That's oddly specific.

Cass:

See you tonight! Tell Amelia to think of what song she wants to do. If she's coming to open mic, she's getting up there.

I study my screen. Cass ignoring a question isn't new; it happens any-time I mention her childhood. She's told me little snippets of information about her parents, but nothing concrete. Enough to think her childhood wasn't great.

It's her use of my kid's full name that has me confused. I decide to go straight to the source and knock on the bathroom door in the upstairs hallway. "Mellie?"

"You can come in!" I open the door to find her with half of her long blonde hair piled on top of her head as she rubs pink stuff all over the lower half. She meets my eye in the mirror. "Did Cass say I can go?"

"Yes. She said to think about what song you want to sing." Mellie's eyes shine with excitement. "She called you Amelia in the text. Kinda weird, huh?" I see the flash of nervousness take over, but she doesn't respond. "I'm not sure I've ever heard anyone call you Amelia other than your mom."

Mellie mumbles under her breath, but it's too quiet for me to make out what she's saying. I have my suspicions, but I want to hear her say it.

"What did you say?"

"Everyone at school calls me Amelia," she declares with a defiant expression on her face.

"Why would they call you by your full name?"

"Because it's how I introduced myself. I want to go by Amelia."

I chuckle. "Was that so hard? It's been months; why am I the last to know about this switch?"

She shrugs. "I wasn't sure you'd be willing to change what you call me. You've always called me Mellie unless I was in trouble."

"Sweetie. Your mom and I chose the name Amelia because we liked it. We called you Mellie because Amelia felt too serious for a tiny baby, and then we never broke the habit. If you want to switch to Amelia, it's fine with me. I don't care what you call yourself, I'll always support you, but you gotta tell me these things."

"It was the one thing I could control. I didn't get a say in anything with the divorce and moving here... I just wanted something that was mine."

I blow out a big breath and move to sit on the closed toilet so I can watch her while she continues to coat her hair in pink. "I'm sorry, kiddo. I'm sorry this has all been hard on you, but you know your mom and I were only doing things we thought were best for our family, right?"

"I know. Cass and I were talking about it the other day."

"You were?" I do my best to keep my voice even despite my curiosity.

"Yeah. Well, we were talking about names 'cuz Cass is a nickname, and she hates her full name. Which makes total sense because it doesn't fit her at all and she—"

"Wait, what's Cass's full name?" I interject, unable to stop myself.

"Nuh-uh, I pinkie promised I wouldn't tell anyone."

"Come on. Not even me?"

"Nope."

"What if I paid you?"

Amelia's eyebrows wing up as she turns to study my face. "Why do you want to know so bad?"

I shrug and drop eye contact, hoping my thirteen-year-old isn't observant enough to catch on to why I want this information. "It would be fun to be in on the secret."

"How much are we talking?"

"Twenty bucks?"

Amelia laughs out loud. "You'll have to do better than that if you want me to break a pinkie promise with Cass. She's a badass. She'd probably make me scrub the Café's trash cans or toilets or something."

I laugh at her assessment of Cass. "She's a tough one all right."

"I think she had to be."

A chill goes down my spine at Amelia's tone. "What do you mean?"

She swallows hard, her voice barely a whisper when she answers, "I think her parents were bad. We were talking about it, and Cass kinda zoned out. She had an awful look on her face, and I practically had to yell her name to get her to snap out of it. It was scary."

My hands clench into fists at the idea of anyone mistreating Cass. Her own parents might have hurt her, and it makes my blood boil. It would also explain quite a lot about why she's so closed off. "Did she say anything else about them?"

"No, once we changed the subject, she went back to normal." Amelia shrugs and focuses back on coating the rest of her hair in pink chalk.

I'm about to ask more questions when the doorbell rings. Drew races down the stairs to open it for Nessa.

"I'll let your mom know why you're not going with them, but you should come and say hi before they leave."

"Okay, I'll be right there."

I make my way down the stairs to find my ex-wife dressed in a full pirate costume, complete with drawn-on facial hair. She's wearing a bald cap over her hair, clearly waiting to add the hat and Captain Hook's curly wig until she's at the event.

"Excuse me, sir, why are you in my house?" I ask in a mock-serious tone.

"Ha ha, you're hilarious," Nessa deadpans. "Where's Mellie?"

"Well, first, she's decided she wants to be called Amelia. She's apparently been introducing herself as Amelia at school."

Nessa's eyebrows wing up, and she nods. "Okay. I take it from your tone that this is an important development."

"Yeah, I'll fill you in more later. Also, she's staying here this weekend." Nessa's face falls, but I shake my head with a smile. "No, Ness, she got invited to go trick-or-treating with the girls in her class." I wiggle my eyebrows at her in excitement.

"Oh, that's great!" Relief floods Nessa's face. We've both been pretty worried Amelia's transition to Fort Starling wasn't going well.

Before we can say any more, Amelia comes bouncing down the stairs, hair completely pink, wearing a yellow jean skirt, a cropped black tee, and tall boots. I bite my tongue to not object to the costume and insist she put more clothing on. I can't believe my mother sent her this costume.

"Hi there, demon hunter!" Nessa calls out.

Amelia rolls her eyes but smiles. "Hi, Mom. Did Dad tell you I'm gonna stay here? Is that okay?" She nervously tucks her pink hair behind her ears.

"It's fine, sweetie. I hope you have fun with your friends. Peter Pan and Captain Hook gotta get going!" Nessa winks at Amelia and grabs Drew's bag. "Pan, say goodbye to Dad and Amelia."

Amelia stands up a little straighter at Nessa using her preferred name, and Drew barrels into me, hugging me quickly before running out the front door. "Bye, Dad! Bye, Mellie!"

Nessa gives Amelia a quick hug and waves at me as she follows Drew out the door. I shrug at Amelia. "Drew might take a little practice to get the name switch down."

"Eh, it's okay, I figured he wouldn't really get it."

"You never know, he may want to switch to Andrew," I joke.

She gives me a sheepish smile. It's the happiest she's looked in a while, and some of the tension I've been holding since we moved here eases.

"What time are you meeting your friends?"

"They're gonna be here just before trick-or-treat starts at six." She looks down at her phone. "So, half an hour."

"Okay, I'm gonna go get my costume on, and then we can set up our candy table in the driveway so I can meet your friends when they come around."

"Please don't embarrass me."

"*What?* Me?" I say sarcastically. Amelia rolls her eyes and buries her face back into her phone. I chuckle to myself and go back up the stairs to put on my costume. Her teenage attitude is strong, but she's finally showing signs she's gonna be okay here.

"I can't believe you left the house like that, Dad. Who even are you?"

My jaw drops, and I pinch the bridge of my nose. "I have failed as a father. How do you not know who Han Solo is? Did I never make you watch *Star Wars?*"

"Uh, I think we watched it; I just didn't care." She shrugs like she's not breaking my elder millennial heart.

"Well, I know what we're doing tomorrow," I say as I open the door to the Songbird, music pouring out of the door. Open mic is already underway since we stopped to grab food on the way. On stage, there's an older man dressed in a very elaborate Michael Jackson costume singing "Thriller."

Amelia giggles when she sees him. "It's Fred! He was here the other day. He's so nice. I think he's like Aunt Leena's grandpa or something."

The older man is doing a pretty good moonwalk before going back into the choreography from the music video. "He's pretty good!"

Bailey waves at us from a table near the front. It's a perfect spot between the stage and the bar, and we make our way over. Bailey is dressed as Fiyero from *Wicked,* and a quick scan of the bar is all it takes to find Leena wearing a full face of green makeup. She makes her way over with Annie and Eric, who are dressed as Buttercup and Wesley from *The Princess Bride*.

Leena stops in her tracks when she sees me and narrows her eyes. "You didn't. Did you clear this costume with Cass?"

"Does that sound like a Han Solo move? He's definitely more of an 'ask forgiveness instead of permission' sort of guy." I smirk, and Leena shakes her head at me.

"Your funeral, man."

"I did bring her a bowl from Piada as a peace offering."

Leena huffs out a laugh. "The pasta might actually save your ass. She loves Piada."

"What's she talking about, Dad?" Amelia asks from her seat as she opens her pasta bowl. I don't have time to answer before I hear Cass's angry voice.

"Are you kidding me?"

I'm already smiling when I turn around to find her in the full-length white, draped Princess Leia dress with braided buns on the sides of her head. "I like your costume, Your Worshipfulness."

Cass crosses her arms and narrows her eyes, and I don't know whether she's actually pissed or channeling Carrie Fisher.

"Cass, who are you dressed as?" Amelia chimes in, and Cass's eyebrows wing upward. She immediately snaps back to look at me.

"How does your kid not recognize Princess Leia? What kind of dad are you?" she jokes, nudging my arm with hers, reassuring me she's not *too* pissed I surprised her with a couple's costume.

"We're fixing that tomorrow. We're bingeing at least the original trilogy," I say with determination. Amelia rolls her eyes and huffs.

"Why don't we do it here?" Cass asks. "We have a projector screen we've used for movies before."

"Yes!" Leena chimes in. "We can do a whole day of *Star Wars* bingeing like the girl on Threads. Daddy smut, or smut father, or something like that! The one who was watching it for the first time."

"Oh my God, yeah! I remember that. Her posts were so much fun to follow along with!" Annie chimes in.

As soon as Cass and the girls are the ones to suggest it, Amelia suddenly changes her tune. "It would be so much fun! Can we, Dad?"

"Oh, now you want to watch it? When I suggested it, you just rolled your eyes."

"Well, yeah, but it would be more fun to watch it here with everyone."

I huff a laugh at her polite way of saying she didn't want to hang out with just me, and agree we can spend the day at Songbird. As soon as Amelia is distracted, chatting with Bailey about school, I murmur to Cass, "Thank you."

She shoots me a look that says she knows exactly what I mean, but still asks, "For what?"

"You knew she was gonna blow me off and offered to watch the movies here." I turn my head to look at her, and she rolls her lips in, trying to hide a smirk.

She shrugs. "The child clearly needs to be educated. Didn't fucking recognize Princess Leia. And don't think you're off the hook for this couple's costume ambush." She gestures at my costume but takes her time with a slow perusal of it, head to toe.

"You can punish me for it later, Spitfire."

I don't miss the fire that flares in Cass's eyes and file it away for future reference. "In the meantime, I brought you pasta. I texted Bailey for your Piada order and everything."

"Fine, you're forgiven for now, but you're on thin ice, flyboy."

"I'll take it," I say, grinning down at her.

For once, she gives me a full, radiant smile, and my entire chest squeezes with how much I'm falling for this woman. I can only hope she's falling for me, too.

Cass joins the table, taking a seat next to Amelia, and they instantly fall into comfortable chatter. Sometimes I forget how much time Cass spends with my kid. Sitting on the other side of Amelia, I watch the two interact while I quietly eat my meal. They're so natural together, you'd think they had been friends for years. I can't help but picture them years from now as more than friends. As a family.

Cass and I aren't even officially dating, but I can't quite keep my brain from imagining a future together. I have no idea how she feels about marriage or kids, but fuck if I don't want her for the long haul. It's a conversation we'll have to have at some point, but for now I'm going to hold on to the vision and hope someday it could come true.

Chapter Twelve

Cass

GRIFFIN IS WEARING ME down. I'm holding onto my walls and armor with both hands, but he's tearing them down bit by bit with every passing day.

I have dressed up as Princess Leia for Halloween for more years than I can even count. I've never wanted someone to dress up as Han Solo with me. But somehow, Griffin showing up in the signature leather jacket and tight pants has unlocked something in me. He asked me the week before Halloween what my costume plans were. I thought he was just making conversation, but he was actually making a plan to surprise me.

He's been doing this kind of thing often in the last couple of weeks since Halloween. I'll mention something in passing—a snack, a song, a show—and the next thing I know, he's bringing me my favorite candy or sending me a funny meme from the show I just finished watching. It's endearing in a way I've never encountered before.

It would help if the sex weren't so spectacular, but it only gets better every time. I seriously underestimated the power of someone who's taken the time to learn what I like and can get me there in record time. Even if things don't work out with Griffin, he's made me completely reevaluate what I want in life.

"Cass, you okay?" I blink out of my spiraling thoughts at Leena's voice. The hairstylist is still pinning my curled hair, so I don't shake my head like I want to. I glance up at Leena as best I can.

"Shouldn't I be asking you that? It's your wedding day."

Leena laughs and shrugs. "Maybe if I weren't one thousand percent sure Bailey is the one I want to spend the rest of my life with, it would be valid." She gives me a dazzling smile, reminding me of a fairy princess with her vibrant red hair curled around her shoulders, a crown of flowers decorating the top of her head. "You're the one who looks like you want to make a run for it."

I blow out a big breath of air and peek around the room to see where our other friends are. Both Annie and Jessie are occupied making faces at Jessie's three-week-old daughter, with Jessie's mother-in-law standing ready for baby duty.

"I think I'm in over my head with Griffin," I say, my voice barely above a whisper.

"I knew there was something more going on! Halloween kind of gave it away." Leena smirks at me and waggles her eyebrows suggestively.

"He did not clear the couple's costumes with me!"

She laughs and shakes her head. "No, I meant the way you were looking at each other all night. The next day at the *Star Wars* party, too. You guys aren't nearly as subtle as you think you are." I groan, wanting to bury my face in my hands, but I don't want to mess up the nice lady doing my hair. "So what's the problem?"

"I'm in over my head. We haven't put any labels on what we're doing, but it's been a month, and he wants to be more. He wants to tell people we're together. Tell the kids. I don't know how to do any of this!"

"Breathe, babes. I think you're making this more complicated than it needs to be. You like spending time with him, right?"

"Yes. More than I thought possible."

"Okay. Good. You like spending time with the kids, right?"

I purse my lips, seeing where she's going. "I mean, I haven't been around Drew much, but I'm close with Amelia."

"Drew's a little sweetheart; there won't be any problems there. So you like spending time with Griffin and his kids, what's the problem?"

"I don't know how to be in a relationship."

Leena scoffs. "Babes, you're already in one. What do you think will change when you make it official? I can guarantee Griffin doesn't have a list of separate expectations for a girlfriend versus whatever you're doing now. The only thing that will change is you won't have to sneak around anymore."

I open my mouth to argue and then snap it closed, knowing she's probably right. I wrack my brain for some kind of justification for my panic, some legitimate reason to be taking a step back. "What if he wants to get married?"

"Pretty premature to be worrying about him wanting to get married when you won't even let yourself openly date him." She makes a funny face at me, trying to dispel the tension I'm radiating into the room.

"I'm not stepmom material," I blurt.

"Says fucking who? You're great with Amelia. You're amazing with Meg's little boy."

"What if he wants more kids? I definitely don't want to be an actual mom. I can barely stomach the idea of being a stepmom."

"I will once again point out, you're getting way ahead of yourself. You're trying to talk yourself out of something good. Listen to me, Cass." She leans down so we're face-to-face, and I don't have a choice but to look into her hazel eyes. "I know exactly what it's like to be terrified of putting yourself out there. I get it more than most people would, and I distinctly remember *you* telling me to stop hiding from my feelings and to be honest with myself. It's time for you to take your own advice."

I swallow hard, closing my eyes to contain the emotions bubbling to the surface. The hairstylist, who I'll assume was eating up the drama of our conversation, tells me she's done with my hair. I thank her and turn back to Leena, who's smiling warmly at me.

I finally find my voice. "Thank you, Leens." I reach out and pull her into a hug that surprises her, since I'm usually not much of a hugger. "Now enough about me, let's go get you married."

THE CEREMONY WAS GORGEOUS, and man, did I forget how good Griffin looks in a suit. I did my best to stay focused on Leena and Bailey, but my gaze kept wandering to Griffin standing next to his brother. I'd be embarrassed about my wandering eyes, but I found him already staring at me more often than not.

More than once, he's shot me a smug wink when he catches me looking his way, and I roll my eyes back at him. Leena even makes the photographer take a picture of the two of us together. I tried to argue, but she just raised her eyebrows as if she were daring me to say out loud that we weren't together. Annie and Jessie snickered at us from the sidelines, clearly in on the joke.

Once we were in the reception hall, I could put a little more space between us through dinner, but I can feel his gaze on me as I move around the room now that the dancing is starting.

Fred and Leena are in the center of the dance floor for the father-daughter dance. He stepped in since Leena's parents died when she was little, and he's the closest she has to family. He and his wife were good friends with Leena's gram, who raised her.

I'm doing my best not to get emotional as I watch, when Jessie appears at my side, flustered. "Cass! Can you hold Lottie for a second? I have to pee so bad, and I can't find Marlene or Dan!"

"Oh, uh, sure," I mumble as I take the squirming baby Jessie hands me. She looks adorable in her frilly flower girl dress and sparkly headband. I arrange her in my arms so she's more comfortable, and I bounce to the beat of the music to keep her from being pissed that her mama walked away.

Kids are not usually my thing. I didn't babysit as a teenager, and I have never felt the urge to procreate myself. But I spent a lot of time around Beckett over the last four years, so I can handle a baby even if it's not my first choice activity.

I can feel Griffin's gaze before I find him across the room, standing with Amelia and his mom, Pam. I met her earlier in the day by accident, but she didn't act like she knew about me and Griffin. She seems like a really nice lady. Nothing like my mom.

Griffin's staring me down with a strange look on his face I can't quite read. Before I can think too much about it, Lottie fusses, recapturing my attention. I bounce and sing her the song the DJ is playing until Jessie comes back to claim her.

By the time I look for him, Griffin's being dragged away by the groomsmen for a cigar outside, so I hit the dance floor with Amelia. We're doing a poor version of the choreography for Taylor Swift's "The Fate of Ophelia" when I find Amelia studying me.

I raise my eyebrows at her while we dance. "What's up, kid?"

"Are you dating my dad?"

I freeze for just a second, staring at her wide-eyed. Griffin would be cool with telling her the truth, but I don't know if I'm ready. I may not have a choice, though. "What makes you ask?"

Amelia rolls her eyes and shrugs. "It's kind of obvious. You keep looking at each other weird. Plus, you had those matching costumes on Halloween. It was super sus."

I huff a laugh. Clearly, we were hiding our relationship from absolutely no one. "How would you feel if I were?"

She shrugs again. "I think you're way too cool for him, but I guess it would be pretty fun if you were around more."

I laugh and fight the tears welling up in my eyes. What have these people done to me? I never used to get teary so easily. I pull Amelia into a side hug. "I'm gonna need you to tell your dad that."

"So I was right? You're my dad's girlfriend?"

I swallow hard before answering. "Yeah, kid. You were right. Apparently, your dad and I aren't very good at keeping a secret."

"No, you're not, but it's cool." She gives me a sheepish smile.

The song shifts to a slower song, and Griffin comes alongside us.

"Amelia, can I steal Cass for a few minutes?"

She rolls her eyes. "Ugh, just don't be gross, Dad."

I laugh, and he raises his eyebrows at me, offering a hand.

"Dance with me, Spitfire?"

Chapter Thirteen

Griffin

I'VE BEEN WATCHING CASS all day, waiting for when I could get my hands on her in the slinky, sage green bridesmaid dress. I was going to steal her from Amelia when I came in from the groomsman's cigar break, but my mom intercepted me. Even while dancing with my mom, I can't keep my eyes off Cass dancing with Amelia.

"I take it you and Cass are a thing?" Her brown eyes twinkle as she looks up at me.

I laugh. "We've officially failed at keeping it to ourselves."

"I'll say. There is nothing subtle in the way you've been looking at each other today. I'm not sure I ever saw you look at Nessa like that." I raise my eyebrows at my mom's assessment. She's always been a big Nessa fan and was disappointed when the divorce happened. "I love Nessa. She gave me two beautiful grandbabies, but I'm seeing the wisdom in her decision."

"I know. I didn't know chemistry like this was a real thing. I thought it was something movies made up." I frown, thinking about how rare this all is.

"So why the sad face? Is it not going well?"

I blow out a big breath. "Well, up to this point, she's refused to even say we're in a relationship. She's so guarded, and every time I think I've broken through her walls, I find a new one."

"I guess you have to keep digging."

"But what if we don't want the same things? We've avoided having any deeper relationship talks about the future. What if we're not on the same page?"

"Same page for what?" she asks, brow furrowed.

I clench my jaw as the image of Cass holding Dan and Jessie's tiny baby fills my brain again. She looked so stunning holding a baby, and it hit me suddenly. Cass is a whole ten years younger than me. Plenty young enough still to want a child of her own.

"What if she wants kids?"

"Well, I certainly hope she does, considering you've got two."

I roll my eyes and huff a frustrated breath. "I meant a kid of her own. What if she wants a baby?"

"Is it a deal-breaker for you?" She raises her eyebrows in question, but luckily with no judgment on her face.

I nod slowly, voicing the thought for the first time. "Yeah, I think so. I don't want to start over. The diapers, the sleepless nights, not to mention juggling having teenagers and a newborn. It sounds like a nightmare."

"It's a conversation you're gonna have to have then. She seems to be bonding well with Amelia, though."

I follow Mom's gaze to find Cass and Amelia sharing a side hug and laughing. The second I see Cass swipe under her eye to clear a tear, I'm pulling away from Mom. I pause and look back at her.

She squeezes my arm. "Go get her, sweetie."

I reach Cass's side just as a slower song comes on and ask Amelia if I can steal Cass away. In typical teenage fashion, she tells me not to be gross, and then I'm finally pulling Cass into my arms like I've been itching to do all day. She takes a quick look around the room.

"I'm pretty sure we're past keeping whatever this is a secret," I murmur into her ear.

She scoffs. "Considering your daughter just asked me if I was dating her dad, I'd say you're right."

I pull back to meet her eyes, tension rolling through my body. "What did you tell her?"

She shrugs and smiles, looping her arms around my neck and eliminating the space between us. "I told her the truth."

"Uh-huh, and what is that exactly?"

She rolls her eyes at me, but I need to hear her say what we are. She smirks and meets my eyes. "She asked if I was her dad's girlfriend..." She trails off, teasing me now.

"And you said..."

She gives me one of her rare, full smiles and threads her fingers through the short hair at the nape of my neck. "I told her I am."

Warmth floods my veins at her words, and the tension escapes my body. I didn't realize how badly I needed her to admit it. How much I wanted to hear those words. I lower my head to rest my forehead against hers.

"I like the sound of that."

"She did say she thought I was too cool for you, but I thought we could just overlook that detail."

I shake my head and chuckle at my own kid's willingness to drag me. "She's probably not wrong."

Cass shrugs. "I like you anyway."

I can't resist dropping my lips to hers, pressing her body into mine with a hand at her lower back. We lose ourselves in the kiss until we hear Amelia hiss, "This is what I meant by not being gross, guys."

We break apart laughing to find Amelia standing next to us with her arms crossed. She is pretending to be mad, but I can see the humor in her eyes. Before she can say anything else sassy, my dad scoops her into his arms and starts dancing with her. He spins her, making her giggle.

"Grandpa!"

"Leave the lovebirds alone, Mell's Bells. Let's go get more cake," he says as he dances them away from us. She rolls her eyes at the nickname he's always used, but goes with him to the cake table.

Cass's eyes follow the two of them until I recapture her attention. "Come home with me tonight?"

"The kids—"

"Are going home with Nessa. It's her weekend, technically." I give her a suggestive smile.

"Shit. I forgot Nessa was here. Will this be weird for her?" Cass starts frantically searching the room for my ex-wife with a worried look on her face.

I grip Cass's chin to draw her focus back to me.

"Nessa has known how I felt about you since before we got together last month. She's still one of my closest friends and is actively rooting for us." I chuckle at the surprised look on her face. "Any other excuses? Because I'm really invested in finally having you in my bed tonight."

Her eyes darken and heat as she swallows hard. She shakes her head slowly, a devious smile crossing her face. "Well, we can't leave yet, whatever will we do in the meantime?"

"Obviously, we're gonna do our best to embarrass my teenager."

Cass laughs as fate, and the DJ, help us out by playing "Hips Don't Lie." I spin her around, moving my hands to rest on her hips, just like the first night so many months ago. I lean down to murmur in her ear, "What are the chances of them playing our song?"

Cass shakes her head, and I can feel her body shake with laughter. "It's been on Leena's must-play list since college. I insisted on it at every party."

Sure enough, my new sister-in-law makes a beeline for us across the dance floor, arms in the air and hips swaying. Bailey trails after her, smiling at his bride's antics. Annie and Eric join right away and are followed by an exhausted but happy-looking Dan and Jessie.

As my gaze sweeps the room, I can't help but be overcome by how right this feels. Cass dancing in my arms, surrounded by people who are quickly becoming my close friends, with my family dancing and laughing across the room. For this moment, everything feels perfect.

I knew when we moved to Fort Starling, it was the right move for Nessa and the kids, but now I'm seeing just how right it was for *me*. I had no idea my dream life would be here waiting for me, and I'll do whatever it takes to keep it.

"Do you need anything from your apartment?" I ask Cass as I open the car door for her to slide in. I hand her the giant tote bag I had to fight her to carry as she gets settled in her seat.

She pats the bag. "No, I have half the contents of my apartment in this bag. The girls picked me up at the ass crack of dawn, so I had to make sure I had all the toiletries, clothing, and snacks I could possibly need for today. I could probably make it a month before going back to my apartment."

I shoot her a mischievous grin. "You're welcome to stay at my place as long as you'd like, but the kids will be back tomorrow night."

Cass rolls her eyes. "Let's not get ahead of ourselves here. It's one thing for them to know I'm your girlfriend. I don't think I'm ready for family sleepovers just yet."

I chuckle, but my heart squeezes both at the sound of the label and the hope she's not ruling out the possibility of eventually becoming a more permanent fixture of my family. I can already see it so clearly in my mind if she would let herself be open to it.

We drive in peaceful silence through the clear night for a while before she asks, "Does it feel weird to be a boyfriend again when you used to be someone's husband?"

Her voice is light, as if it's just a random thought and not a loaded question. I don't think she's doubting our labels, so I answer honestly. "A little. I feel too old to be a boyfriend." She snickers, and I shoot her a dirty look. "But boyfriend feels better than not having a label."

She hums in response and looks out the window. When I park in my garage, I get up the courage to ask, "Does it feel weird to be someone's girlfriend?"

She turns in her seat and studies my face. I'm not sure what she finds there, but her eyes soften, and she smiles. "Not as weird as I thought it would be."

I lean across the center console to kiss her, and she immediately moves to deepen the kiss. Before we can get carried away, I pull back and open my door. "No more car sex. I swear my back is permanently damaged from that time last week."

She laughs as she opens her door, and I hustle around the front of the car to help her out and carry her bag. I guide her into the house, not bothering to flick on the lights in the kitchen as we pass through. I pull her quickly toward the stairs that lead to my bedroom.

"You're not gonna give me a tour?" she teases.

I turn and face her at the base of the stairs, threading my hand into her curled updo falling out of the pins. "Spitfire, I've been imagining peeling you out of this silky dress and finding out what you're wearing underneath since the moment I saw you this afternoon. I can give you a tour later."

She swallows hard, and I know her cheeks are tinged with pink even though I can't see it in the house's dimness. She tips her head toward the stairs.

"Lead the way. But for the record..." She leans toward me, lowering her voice to a conspiratorial whisper. "I'm not wearing anything under this dress."

Her words flood my brain with heat as I study her smug look. My inner caveman roars to life. In a flash, I drop her tote bag to the floor and bend to hoist Cass over my shoulder. She lets out a very un-Cass-like noise that's half shriek, half giggle as I take off up the stairs toward my bedroom.

Chapter Fourteen

Cass

GRIFFIN'S SUDDEN NEANDERTHAL ROUTINE should not be turning me on as much as it is. If I had underwear on, they would be soaked.

"Put me down!" I squirm as he readjusts his hold on me at the top of the stairs. He brings his big hand down on my ass with a resounding smack that makes me gasp and makes my core clench.

Christ. This man. He chuckles at my reaction to the spanking and kicks the door to the bedroom closed behind us. "If I let you down, can you be a good girl?"

I whimper rather than respond, and he gives me another swat. "What did you say?"

"Yes, please," I whine before he lowers me, letting my body slide down the front of his to stand on my bare feet, my shoes discarded when we came in the door. I stand on my tiptoes to connect my lips to his in a searing kiss that has him groaning into my mouth.

His hands grip my ass, his fingers bunching the silky material of the floor-length satin gown as he pulls our bodies flush together. We stay here, devouring each other for what feels like an hour but is probably only a couple of minutes. When he travels his kisses down the side of my neck, sliding the thin straps of my dress down off my shoulders, I reach up to unbutton his dress shirt.

Griffin finds the zipper hidden on the side of my dress and yanks it down, loosening it enough for it to drop to the floor. Between the cups built into the bodice of the dress and the clingy fabric, I wasn't joking about being completely bare beneath it. I straighten and take a small step back.

Griffin's gaze tracks down my body as he blows out a shaky breath. For all the hooking up we've done over the last few weeks, it's been rare for either of us to be fully naked. Quickies and car sex don't really lend themselves to stripping down to nothing, and now I find myself craving full skin-on-skin.

I rush forward to undo his belt as he unbuttons the cuffs of his sleeves and ditches his shirt. We make quick work of his pants and briefs, his dick bouncing up between us. Once he's as naked as I am, I waste no time in pressing our bodies together, pulling him back down to link our mouths.

His hands thread through my hair, pulling at the pins holding the curls down. I enjoy the sharp pain of it, and my pussy pulses, desperate to be filled. We make our way down to the bed without breaking apart. The tip of his erection grazes right where I need him. He tips his hips away, and I whine at the loss.

"Griffin, please, I need to feel you." I wrap my hand around his length, bringing him back to my entrance.

He makes a strangled noise against my lips and murmurs, "Condom?"

Up to this point, we've used them every time. We had a conversation about them early on, and I requested we continue to use them despite us both being all-clear on the testing front. I wasn't ready to explain why pregnancy is a non-issue for me. Plus, not using a condom felt so official. Intimate in a way I wasn't prepared for.

But now.

"I'm good going without, if you are," I whisper.

Griffin pulls back to study my face. He must be able to read my sincerity because he exhales sharply and lowers his forehead to mine. Without a word, he reaches between us to line himself up, pressing into me slowly.

We both let out soft moans as he fills and stretches me with his hard length. Whether it's the lack of a condom or the progress our relationship has made today with becoming official, I'm overcome with emotion. Every sensation is heightened as he picks up the pace, pistoning his hips into me, gaining speed.

"Fuck, Cass. You feel so incredible," Griffin moans into my hair.

"I'm already close," I whimper, surprised by how quickly my orgasm is barreling toward me.

Griffin snakes his hand between us to circle my clit with his fingertips without slowing his thrusts.

I grind my hips into his fingers, seeking the pressure I need to detonate.

"Come for me, honey, I've got you."

At his words, I shatter, my release taking over and making my vision go white. Griffin doesn't slow down as he fucks me through the orgasm.

"Christ. Your pussy's squeezing my dick so fucking tight," he growls. He shifts, bringing his hand to grip my hip as he pounds into me, losing control of his rhythm.

I wrap my legs around him, pulling him deeper. It doesn't take long before a second orgasm is closing in.

"Give me one more, Spitfire. Milk me with this tight pussy." His filthy mouth tips me over the edge.

I decide to return the favor with some choice words of my own. "Griffin, I want you to come inside me."

With a guttural moan, he stiffens, his whole body going rigid as he does exactly what I asked for. He collapses onto me, and I revel in his comforting weight. "Oh my god. That was... I can't even..." he stammers into my ear, unable to find words and I huff a laugh.

"Same."

We stay linked for a few moments before he gently pulls out. Our releases mix and flow down the inside of my thighs in a sensation that's not completely pleasant. Griffin grabs a tissue from the box on the nightstand and gently cleans the mess.

"Come on, honey, let's get cleaned up."

He carries me again, this time cradled in his arms, to the bathroom. He sets me on the edge of a large jacuzzi tub that I fully intend to use sometime soon as he starts the shower. I yank the pins out of my hair as I watch Griffin bustle around the bathroom, grabbing towels and checking the water. He seems nervous for some reason.

Once the last pin has been removed, I stand and move to the shower. I glance over my shoulder to find Griffin watching me with a worried look on his face.

"You comin'?" I ask, eyebrows raised in question.

He nods and follows me into the large, tiled shower. I scrape my nails along my scalp, hissing at the pain the bobby pins have left behind. I can feel Griffin standing near me, but he's not touching me. When I open my eyes to find him watching me with the same wary expression, I start to panic.

Is he having second thoughts about us? With how serious everything's gotten today, is he realizing I'm not what he wants?

"What's wrong?" I whisper when the intrusive thoughts get to be too much.

He sighs. "Sorry. I guess... I was half-expecting you to want some space with everything today."

Shit. He's not changing his mind, but he's afraid I'll change mine. I gotta get my shit together. Some aspects of an actual relationship may still freak me out, but I don't want him to think I've constantly got one foot out the door. I can't promise him forever yet, but I want to give this—us—a real chance.

I close the distance between us, looping my arms around his middle and resting my head on his shoulder. We fit so perfectly together.

"I don't want space," I murmur into the skin of his collarbone.

The tension in his body relaxes a bit, and he wraps his arms around me and places a tender kiss on my forehead. "I promised we could take things slow. Then, all in one day, we made our relationship official and told everyone we know about us. Plus, just now... It's all been intense, and I was worried it was too much."

I squeeze him just a little bit tighter. "It has been intense. But... it all felt... right, somehow?"

He blows out a shaky breath and relaxes more. "I think so, too." He drops his head against mine, and we stay locked together for several minutes, holding each other in the warm spray. The exhaustion of the long day takes over, and we wash quickly, sharing soft touches and smiles as we dry off and get ready for bed.

Before I fall asleep, wrapped in Griffin's arms and wearing his shirt, I find myself hoping desperately I can be what he needs.

A FEW DAYS LATER, I'm at Leena's house doing Thanksgiving prep. Annie and Jessie are here helping, too. Leena found out at the beginning of the month that she's pregnant. Luckily, she made it through the wedding fine, but the fatigue has hit her hard this week, so we're all teaming up to get our Friendsgiving ready. She asked me to make my family's Puerto Rican-style turkey for the meal tomorrow, so I'm busy chopping peppers, onions, green olives, mushrooms, garlic, and cilantro to stuff into the turkey's meat.

"Cass, I seriously can't wait to have this turkey tomorrow! I think I've been craving it since you made it a couple of years ago," Leena says from where she's sitting at the counter, drinking a ginger ale after a nausea spell hit her a few minutes ago.

I chuckle. "It might be one of my favorite foods ever. We always had it this way growing up."

"I'm excited to try it! My mom raved about it the year you made it," Annie chimes in. "I was still in Chicago, and I never really bothered with a full Thanksgiving meal since it was just me. I would make a green bean casserole and buy a pumpkin pie and call it a day."

We've been doing our Friendsgiving on Thanksgiving Day for several years now. Since none of us really had family nearby, it made sense. Jessie's like me and doesn't speak to her family, so we've all leaned into our little friend group. It used to make me kind of uncomfortable. I was always more Leena's friend, whereas the rest of them have been friends since middle school, but this year I feel a little closer to all of them.

"Jessie, who has the baby today?" Leena asks.

"She's with Dan, and I think Marlene was gonna be around, but I know she's busy making food to bring over tomorrow. I needed a little break, and I was able to pump some milk for her." She smiles with so much love in her eyes that it makes my chest ache. "I love being her mom, but I needed a couple of hours away."

"Makes sense. I'm glad you could take a break," Annie squeezes Jessie's hand, and they smile at each other. Jessie looks tired but happy. She turns her eyes to me.

"Cass, you and Griffin looked awfully cozy at the wedding." She waggles her eyebrows suggestively. "Are you finally admitting you're together?"

I roll my eyes, but I can't quite keep the smile off my face at the thought of Griffin. "Yes, we're officially together and not keeping it a secret anymore."

"I knew it! Dan and I overheard you fighting at our baby shower, plus the whole 'Bring On the Men' stunt, so I knew something was going on with you guys." She claps her hands excitedly. "Tell us everything."

I groan and eye the ceiling, gathering my strength for the interrogation I knew was coming today. I fill Jessie and Annie in on the details of how Griffin and I met, thinking it would be a one-night thing, and how he turned out to be Bailey's brother. They both stare wide-eyed at me as I recount the story.

"Whoa. So how's it going now?" Annie asks. "You guys looked so cute together on Saturday."

I sigh. "Griffin and I are really good together. I want it to work between us, but... I don't know. I'm having a hard time figuring out how this works long term."

"Why?" Leena looks confused. "What's the problem?"

I blow out a big breath. "I've never wanted kids. They've always been an absolute deal-breaker in my mind. I'm not cut out to be a mom."

"Does Griffin want more kids?" Jessie asks.

"We haven't had a conversation about it yet, but if he does, it's not something I can do. Literally."

"What do you mean?"

I brace myself to tell them the one thing I've never told anyone. "I had my tubes removed a few years ago. I wanted to permanently make sure I never got pregnant." I knew the last time I dealt with my mom after my dad's funeral, I would never risk becoming her. I never really wanted kids, so it wasn't a hard decision.

When I look up, I'm met with three surprised faces.

"Wow. I had no idea. Why didn't you tell me?" Leena asks, concern on her face.

I shrug. "It was just after my dad died, you were taking care of your Gram and engaged to that asshat. You had a lot going on."

"Still. I wish I had been there for you." She reaches over and squeezes my forearm.

"You're gonna have to tell Griffin," Jessie says. "It was a totally valid decision you made for yourself, but you've gotta be honest with him before things get more serious."

"You think it was a valid decision, Jessie? You don't think I'll change my mind?" I raise my eyebrows at her.

"Why would I think you'd change your mind?" Jessie looks confused.

"That's kind of why we weren't really friends in college. We had an entire argument my freshman year about wanting kids someday, and you condescendingly told me I'd change my mind."

"Shit, Cass. I don't remember that at all. But... honestly, it sounds like me back then. I had a hard time understanding people who wanted different things from me. It probably felt like you were telling me *I shouldn't* want kids. I'm sorry."

Some of the armor I'd built up around myself with Jessie falls away at her words. "It was a long time ago. And I definitely didn't change my mind."

"Totally valid. Having been pregnant and now with a newborn, this is not something I recommend unless you really want to."

"Hard agree." Leena groans from where she's leaning on the countertop.

"Okay, so you'll need to discuss with Griffin that there will be no future babies, but what about the two kids he already has? Are they a deal-breaker?"

"It's part of why I've been so hesitant, why I completely wrote Griffin off at the beginning. But I've really bonded with Amelia, and Drew is so sweet. Anyone else and I would have said yes, kids are a deal breaker, but I can just about wrap my head around Griffin's."

"So you could be okay with being a stepmom but not having a kid of your own. I think that's fair," Annie sums it up with a nod.

"Plus, it's not like Griffin's kids are little babies. They're thirteen and nine, with two very involved and loving parents. Being their stepmom would be similar to being a very involved, fun aunt. I know you enjoy being an auntie for Meg's little boy," Leena points out. "But you still need to have this entire conversation with Griffin. Sooner rather than later."

I nod, feeling relieved at having hashed this all out with the girls. I assure them I'll talk to him about it, and we go back to working on getting the food prepped to be cooked in the morning.

Regardless of how the talk goes with Griffin, I'm thankful for the friendships I've made with these women. It makes me feel like maybe I'm not completely broken after all.

Chapter Fifteen

Griffin

THANKSGIVING PASSES IN A family and friend-filled blur at Bailey and Leena's house. It might be the best Thanksgiving I've had. My parents stuck around after the wedding the weekend before. It made sense for them to stay for the holiday and to do some house hunting. With all of us living here in Fort Starling and a new grandbaby on the way, they're making the move in the new year.

I loved watching Cass interact with my parents, my kids, and even Nessa. I was filled with an overwhelming hope I was getting a glimpse at our future, but in the couple of weeks since, Cass has still avoided coming around when the kids are home. She hangs out with Amelia all the time at the Songbird, but family time still seems to make her nervous, and I don't want to push her.

I feel like I'm on the cusp of having everything I want, but the pieces aren't quite lined up yet. Considering how skittish Cass was about even starting a relationship, I'll take what I can get for now.

"Okay, guys, I think that just about wraps things up," my manager says at the head of the conference room table, pulling me back into the present. "Oh, wait! Kyle is out on paternity leave, so we need to discuss coverage for his clients. It should be fairly quiet, but just in case."

I startle at the new information, but we quickly discuss coverage for Kyle's clients and end the meeting. I hang back until it's just my buddy, Noah, and me in the conference room. We both usually work from home, so the conference room becomes our workspace when we're in the office.

"I didn't know Kyle's wife was expecting. Isn't he older than us? Doesn't he have teenagers?" I ask in a low voice. I'm pretty sure he has a boy a year or two older than Amelia.

Noah chuckles and leans back in his chair. "He does, but he got remarried last summer. His new wife is only thirty and hadn't had kids yet, so he's starting over with a new baby."

I'm quiet for a long moment. *Shit.* That hits close to home.

"Griffin? You okay, man?"

"Uh, yeah. My girlfriend is thirty and doesn't have kids yet. We, um, haven't discussed the idea, and I'm realizing we probably should have."

"Yikes. You gonna be the next one out on paternity leave?"

I groan. "I really don't want more kids."

"I guess you need to have a little chat with your lady friend," he snarks.

"I know. I'm just afraid of spooking her with talk of kids. We're still pretty new."

"That's fair, but I wouldn't wait too long. If you guys aren't on the same page with this, it'll only make things worse if you wait until you're both really attached."

I hum a response. I don't need to admit I'm already really attached to Cass. I'm just afraid the attachment is one-sided, and talk of kids, even saying I don't want more, will send her running.

I do my best to focus on work for the next hour, but really I'm running worst-case scenarios in my head while staring at my laptop.

"Shit. Do you take 70 to get back to Fort Starling?" Noah says suddenly, looking at his phone.

"Yeah, why?"

"The highway's completely shut down. No estimated time of when it'll open."

"Fuck." I pull my phone out to check my route home, and sure enough, it's taking me a roundabout way and will take me nearly three hours instead of the usual hour and a half. "Oh goddammit. I'm not gonna make it back in time to get Drew."

I hit Nessa's contact to see where she's at. If she's already out of the city, we may be okay.

"Hello?"

"Ness, are you still in Columbus or have you already gone home?" I ask, feeling frantic.

"I'm at my office. I don't usually leave for another hour, especially since I don't have the kids. Why, what's wrong?"

"I'm in the office today, and 70 is completely shut down. I can't get back in time to get Drew from his after-school program. Bailey and Leena are still on their honeymoon. *Fuck.*"

"What about Cass? Isn't she already with Amelia?" Nessa asks, voice completely calm and rational.

"She is... we're just... taking things slow when it comes to Cass spending a lot of time with the kids."

Nessa snickers into the phone. "Griff, are you afraid to ask your girlfriend for help watching your kids?"

"No," I say petulantly into the phone.

Nessa laughs. "Listen, you know I am pro-Cass. I think she's great, but if this is going to be a long-term thing with you guys, she's gonna have to get used to hanging out with our kids."

I sigh. "You're right. I've just been trying not to push her too hard, Ness."

"But making it this big, huge deal can't be helping. It's not like you want her to move in and become a stay-at-home mom to a brood of children. You're asking her to pick Drew up and hang out with him and Amelia for a couple of hours. Don't make it bigger than it needs to be."

"I'm gonna call her. I'll let you know what she says."

"I look forward to telling you, 'I told you so!'" Nessa says cheerfully as we disconnect the call. I take a deep breath and dial Cass.

"We were just talking about you!" The warmth and humor in Cass's voice make me smile, despite knowing they were probably making fun of me. I can hear Amelia laughing in the background.

I chuckle. "We're gonna circle back to that, but I actually need a huge favor."

"What's up?" Cass asks casually.

"I'm in the office today, and the highway out of Columbus is completely shut down. Drew needs to be picked up at six, but my ETA is looking like seven-thirty at this point, and I haven't even left yet."

"Shit, that sucks. I can grab him. Is he at the elementary school or somewhere else?"

"I'll send you the address for the theater," I respond, mildly stunned at her lack of hesitation.

"Oh, is he with the Starling Company?" she says calmly.

"Yeah. You know what that is?"

"Griffin, I've lived in Fort Starling for almost four years and have been visiting for a lot longer. Plus, I manage a bar with multiple open mic nights a week and a musical theater-obsessed owner. I'm very aware of the community theater scene here." She chuckles into the phone. "Alaina gets here at five, so it shouldn't be a problem. Wait, does he need a car seat?"

I chuckle. "He's almost ten and is already over five feet, so he's good with just the seatbelt." I can practically hear Cass roll her eyes at me over the phone.

"I don't know his life! I only have experience with my friend's four-year-old, and Meg has talked my ear off about car seat safety and rear-facing seats. I have no frame of reference for nine-year-olds."

"Well, now you do."

"True. So I'll grab Drew and take them to your house. Do they have a key?"

I hear Amelia answering in the background.

"Oh, a keypad, fancy." Cass laughs.

I close my eyes and enjoy listening to them chat. They're so natural together.

"Griffin?"

"Yep, I'm still here. Is this okay? I know it's a huge ask."

"It's really not a big deal. We'll hang out, eat some dinner, make sure any homework is done, and we'll see you when you get through traffic hell."

I huff a laugh, still stunned at how laid-back she's being about spending solo time with my kids, in my house.

"Thanks, Spitfire. I'll see you in a few hours."

"Sounds good."

I end the call and stare at my dark phone screen. The urge to end the phone call with an "I love you" was so strong, I'm not sure how I stopped it from coming out of my mouth.

I start my drive home thinking about the fact that I'm in love with a woman who may not want the same things, and may not be in love with me. It's completely possible I've set myself up for a heartbreak of epic proportions, but I can't justify slowing things down or taking a step back. I'm all in with Cass, and at this point, I have to hope things will work out.

AFTER NEARLY THREE HOURS in the car, I finally pull into my driveway. It's a comforting sight to see the Christmas lights turned on, making the house seem welcoming and cozy from the outside. The second I open the door, I'm hit with the smell of something delicious and the laughter of my favorite people.

Cass is stirring something on the stove, Amelia is scooping rice out of a rice cooker I don't remember having, and Drew is sitting at the table with a steaming bowl in front of him.

He spots me first. "Dad!"

Cass turns and smiles at me, but then turns quickly to Amelia. "I told you I had the timing right!"

Amelia rolls her eyes but smiles at Cass. "Fine, you win." She pulls an extra bowl and glass down from the cabinet to set a place for me at the table. "You couldn't have taken an extra half hour? Now, I have to mop the kitchen at Songbird tomorrow."

I laugh and move toward Cass at the stove. "Sorry, sweetie. I think three hours in the car was plenty. What are you making?"

"The kids said they liked the turkey at Thanksgiving, so we made more Puerto Rican food."

"It smells amazing," I say as I lean in to look in the pot. I can see beef, olives, potatoes, and other vegetables floating in a soup. "What's it called?"

"It probably has a real name, but we always called it 'Puerto Rican food' when my dad made it at home." She shrugs and gives me a sheepish smile.

"Didn't he own a restaurant?" Amelia asks.

Cass chuckles. "He owned a barbecue restaurant with my mom's brother. He was half Puerto Rican and didn't learn to make very many dishes."

"So, are you half Puerto Rican too?" Drew asks, not quite understanding the concept of heritage.

"No, my mom's white, so I'm a quarter. We always jokingly called me a 'Quarter Rican,' so I'm in a weird bracket where I'm not Puerto Rican enough for scholarships or anything but I still check the little 'Hispanic/Latina' box for surveys." Cass shrugs as Amelia hands her the bowls of rice one at a time, and she scoops some of the soup mixture over each.

Amelia takes her bowl to the table and sits next to Drew at the round table, as Cass turns the stove off and covers the soup. It's like they've done this a million times; they're so in sync.

"Do you speak Spanish, Cass?" Amelia asks, continuing the conversation.

"Only what I learned for my minor in college. My dad actually never learned Spanish fully."

"Why not?" Drew asks with his mouth full of rice.

"Things were a little more complicated when he was a kid. Not everyone was super nice to people with darker skin who spoke other languages, so my grandpa didn't want my dad or his sister to learn Spanish. He thought it would make life harder for them. And he might have been right back then, but I know my dad always regretted not learning."

Drew nods his head at this explanation and returns to stuffing his face.

I marvel at Cass's succinct way of explaining something rooted in racism and prejudice in a way a nine-year-old could understand without talking down to him. She's just as natural with Drew as she is with Amelia.

She hands me my bowl and turns off the rice cooker, reminding me to ask, "Did I have a rice cooker?"

Cass shakes her head and chuckles. "No, it's mine. We stopped at my apartment and the grocery store once we had a plan. Amelia had just insisted we didn't need to wait for you to eat and didn't want to set you a place, so I bet her you'd show up right as we were sitting down."

Amelia rolls her eyes, but she has a playful smirk on her face. Cass moves to join the kids, but I grab her hand before she can get far and spin her to face me, careful not to spill the contents of her bowl.

"You know you didn't have to cook, right? We have all kinds of freezer meals the kids like."

She shrugs and smiles. "I wanted to. It sounded good once we started talking about it. Plus, I thought you'd be hungry after battling traffic." She shrugs again, trying to act like going out of her way to make me dinner is no big deal.

I lower my forehead and rest it on hers, breathing her in for a second. "Thank you." I kiss her softly until Amelia yells from the table.

"Stop being gross!"

We both laugh and pull apart. I shoot Cass a wink, and we make our way over to the table to have a family dinner with my kids. It's a scene so perfect it makes my stomach clench with the need to make it permanent.

I just have to make sure Cass wants the same things.

I COME BACK FROM making sure the kids are getting ready for bed to find Cass in the kitchen putting leftovers into containers.

"You really don't need to be cleaning this up when you did all the cooking," I say as I take the pot out of her hand when she dumps the last of the soup into a container. I put it into the dishwasher and start gathering the other dishes.

"I don't mind," she says quietly, smiling up at me.

We work quietly in tandem to clean up the kitchen. Domestic perfection that I hope with all of my soul can become our norm. When we're done, I pull Cass into me as I lean against the counter.

"Thank you again for today. I was panicking when I realized I couldn't get to Drew in time." I loop my arms around her hips, and to my delight, she threads hers around my neck, smiling up at me.

"It really wasn't a big deal," she argues again.

"Yes, it was." I kiss her before she can argue more. "Stay the night?"

She pulls back, unsure. "I don't know. Aren't there rules about not having sleepovers when your kids are here?"

"Only the rules we make," I say with a laugh.

"What about Nessa? Would she be okay with it? You really should discuss it with her first."

"I already did." I grin down at her.

She stiffens and backs a step away, but keeps her hands on my chest. "What? When did you discuss it with her?"

"Just after the wedding. I figured it would happen at some point and wanted us to be on the same page with the kids. She's cool as long as we're discreet where the kids can hear."

Cass's jaw drops in surprise, and I can see her mind spinning to find another reason she shouldn't stay.

"Any other excuses, Spitfire?"

"None I can think of," she grumbles.

I pull her back into me and laugh into the skin along the side of her neck, feeling her body already relaxing into mine. "If you're really uncomfortable with staying, I'll walk you out to your car. But I'd like it if you stayed."

She's quiet for a long moment, studying my face, before she finally nods. "Okay, I'll stay."

I don't dare celebrate my win with anything more than a grin. Even that gets an eye roll out of Cass, so I save the happy dance for later.

"Why don't you go get in the bathtub I saw you eyeing last week while I finish getting the kids down for the night?"

Her eyes light up, and I know instantly I interpreted her lingering look at the jacuzzi tub correctly the other day. It was a safe guess considering she only has a stall shower in her tiny apartment.

"I guess that doesn't sound like a terrible idea," she says with a fake haughty tone.

I pinch her side as she turns away and yank her back into me, kissing her soundly. Her eyes are hazy as I pull back. I slap her ass lightly and push her toward the entrance to the kitchen. "Go get in the tub, and I'll bring you dessert."

"Your kids are here, man, keep it in your pants."

I laugh out loud as she hustles out of the kitchen. I pull out the tray of brownies my mom left when they went back to Portland last week, and cut one big enough for Cass and me to share.

Amelia strolls into the kitchen with her eyebrows raised. "Is Cass spending the night?"

"She is. Is that alright with you?"

She shrugs, but I can see the smile she's trying to hide. "Sure." Amelia leans forward and steals a bite of brownie out of the tray before walking away. At the entrance to the kitchen, she turns her head back toward me and says, "Don't mess it up, Dad."

"I'll do my best, sweetie," I say with a chuckle.

I pop my head into both kids' rooms to say goodnight after locking up the house and turning off the lights. Cass is still in the tub when I step into the bathroom, a layer of fluffy bubbles blocking my view of her body.

Her eyes pop open as she hears me come in. She eyes the brownie in my hand. "You were serious about dessert?" she asks with a smile.

"Of course." I grab a handful of folded towels from the cabinet and make myself a cushion to sit on outside the tub, placing the plate with the brownie on the wide tub edge between us. She sits up to take the fork, and bubbles slide down her breasts, catching my attention.

"Hey, my eyes are up here!" Cass says with a snap.

"I wasn't trying to look at your eyes," I snark back at her, and she chuckles before flicking water at me. "Amelia asked if you were staying the night."

Cass looks up sharply with wide eyes. "She did? What did you tell her?"

"I told her you were and asked if she was okay with it."

"What did she say?"

"She told me 'not to mess it up,'" I say with finger quotes.

Cass barks a laugh. "I love that girl."

My heart rate picks up speed at her casual use of the "L" word, especially since she's saying she loves *my* child. I lose all rational thought and blurt out the words, "Do you want kids?"

She freezes with her fork halfway to her mouth and stares at me. *Fuck.*

Chapter Sixteen

Cass

GRIFFIN'S WORDS RING OUT in the bathroom even though he said them quietly enough. I knew this conversation was coming, but I'm not loving being trapped naked in a tub of water for it. If this doesn't go well, escape will be awkward as fuck.

I set the brownie fork down. "What?" I ask.

"Do you want kids?" he asks again without adding any clarification.

Is he asking about kids of my own or his kids? And are my answers different? *Fuck.* I answer the only way I know how, honestly.

"No."

His eyebrows wing up. "No?"

"No, I don't want to be a mom," I say more strongly. "I never have."

He nods, and I can practically see the thoughts flying behind his eyes. "Okay... what does that mean for us?"

"Well... I guess it depends on whether you want more kids. Do you?"

"No, I really don't."

"Really?"

"No, Amelia and Drew are finally getting more self-sufficient. I can't imagine going back to diapers and spit-up and sleepless nights. Plus, I'm forty. I'd be closing in on my sixties when they hit eighteen."

Some of the tension in my body releases. The baby thing was our biggest hurdle. "Alright, then."

"You really don't want kids of your own?" he asks skeptically.

I chuckle and shake my head. "Hand me a towel, will you? I think I'd rather have some clothing on for this conversation." He chuckles, grabs the brownie, leaving a towel in its place, before stepping out into the bedroom. I drain the tub and quickly dry myself off. Putting on the underwear I luckily had in my purse and one of his shirts, before joining him in the bedroom.

He's perched on the bed, also stripped down to his boxer briefs for bed with the brownie set on the nightstand. He reaches his hand out for me to join him, but I shake my head, slightly moving around to his side of the bed. He sits up on the edge as I come around, and I step between his legs.

I lift the shirt so he can see my lower belly. "Have you ever wondered what these scars are?" I point to the two tiny scars just above the waistband of my underwear.

"I assumed they were something like an appendix surgery or something. I hadn't really thought about it." He lowers his face and gently kisses each scar.

"A few years ago, I had both of my fallopian tubes removed so I would never naturally get pregnant. So, to answer your question, I *really* don't want kids of my own."

He looks up at me, studying my face. A smile grows on his face. "So what you're saying is, we could have ditched the condoms way earlier?"

I bark out a laugh and shove his shoulder. He pulls me down onto his lap, my legs straddling him. Our kiss is passionate with the relief of being on the same page. I notice him hardening beneath me, and I grind my hips down. He thrusts up against me, and a small moan escapes my mouth.

"You're gonna need to be quiet, Spitfire. Do I need to cover your mouth?"

My panties flood with arousal, and I whimper in response. Griffin rolls us so I'm lying flat on the bed and slides his way down my body. He tugs the underwear down my hips and tosses them onto the floor.

Griffin swipes a finger across my clit and through my folds. I gasp, bucking my hips, and he chuckles low. "You're already so wet, you like the idea of me covering your mouth, don't you?"

I squirm and try to swallow the moan that escapes when he slides one long finger inside. He chuckles and snakes his free hand up my body to cover my mouth with his large hand, and I can't hide just how much it turns me on.

He kisses his way down my belly, stopping to place soft kisses on both of my scars before burying his face between my legs. Griffin licks a long swipe along my slit before finding my clit with the tip of his tongue. He swirls his tongue around the tight bud while returning two of his fingers to my core, pumping them deep.

It's a good thing he has my mouth covered because I can't hold back from moaning into his hand. The tension in my body builds unbelievably quickly as he continues using his tongue and fingers to drive me insane.

It doesn't take long before my orgasm is within reach. I lace my fingers into his hair and grind against his face, using the friction of his beard to bring my release closer. He groans against my skin, and the vibration tips me over the edge, sending waves of pure pleasure through my body.

When I've come down from the high, Griffin pulls his hand away from my face and replaces it with his lips in a fervent kiss. The taste of myself on his lips only turns me on again.

"I need to be inside you, honey."

I nod frantically, and he wastes no time in notching his unbelievably hard erection at my entrance and pushing all the way in with one hard thrust. He seals his mouth to mine, swallowing my cries and moans to keep the volume down.

"Fuck. You feel so good. I'm not gonna last long, but I need you to come first."

"I'm so close," I murmur against his lips. My second orgasm takes over, and I whisper, "Come with me."

His body goes taut at my words as he pumps his release inside of me. He lets out a loud groan, and I quickly cover his mouth with my hand. His eyes meet mine, and the heat in them could set the entire house on fire. It looks like I'm not the only one turned on by a little dominance.

He lowers his forehead to rest on mine, and we breathe together, coming down from the intensity of moments ago. How he makes basic missionary into the best sex of my life, I have no idea.

Well... I have an idea, but it's far too intense to give it voice.

Later, once we've cleaned up and finished the brownie, we're snuggled up in bed together. I lay my head on his chest with him running his hand through my hair, when he brings us back to our earlier conversation.

"You said you don't want kids. What about the kids I already have?"

I blow out a big breath. "They're part of why I was so hesitant in starting a relationship. I never saw myself having kids in any way, and with anyone else, they would have been a deal breaker."

"They're not?" Griffin asks tentatively, his muscles tense under me.

I push up so I can look into his eyes. "I happen to really like your kids."

He swallows and pushes my hair behind my ears. "Just the kids?"

I huff a laugh. "Are you fishing for compliments?"

He ignores my attempt at lightening the mood and shakes his head. "I want to hear how you feel."

I study his eyes. "I really like you, too." I can see the relief fill his gaze as I run my hand along his bearded cheek.

"Good," he says in a gruff voice. "I think it's been pretty clear I've been crazy about you since the day we met."

I laugh and drop a light kiss onto his lips. "Very clear."

With soft laughter, we both settle back in for the night. As his breaths even out and his body relaxes, I find myself wide awake and thinking about how quickly life can change.

Less than a year ago, I refused to even sleep with a man more than once to avoid any chance of attachment. Now here I am in a committed relationship, admitting to liking him even though, deep down, it's more. I'm pretty sure I love him, and I have no idea what to do with these feelings.

I'm in so much fucking trouble.

THE HOLIDAYS FLY BY in a blur of holiday song-filled open mic nights and group parties. I spent part of Christmas Day with Griffin and the kids, before they headed to Nessa's for the weekend, and we spent the rest of the holiday just the two of us. On New Year's, we had a big party at the Songbird, and Griffin kissed me at midnight.

We've fallen into a comfortable pattern of me spending several nights a week at his house, and when the kids are at Nessa's house, we spend every minute together. I keep waiting for the panic to take over, but all I feel right now is happy.

Amelia and I are hanging out at the Songbird since she's off from school today for MLK Jr. Day, when Leena pops into the bar.

"Hey girls!" she calls as she crosses the room.

"Hi, Aunt Leena!" Amelia chirps from where she's working on homework.

"How's it been today? Pretty slow?" Leena asks me.

"Yeah, you know how it is on bank holidays. The coffee crowd isn't heading to work, so they don't bother coming in." January is a slow month for us anyway, with the weather and the fact that it gets dark so early keeping people home. Open mic nights pull a bigger crowd. "How you feeling, Leens?"

"I'm finally starting to feel more like myself. Thank God for the second trimester!" she says with a smile. She looks better, less like she's going to need to make a break for the bathroom at any minute. "Of course, the third trimester might kill me. Remember how miserable Jessie was?" She shoots me a wide-eyed look of horror.

"You'll be okay, Leens. Plus, we'll be here to help. I can take on anything extra you need here at the bar."

Leena studies me for a minute. "I actually wanted to talk to you about something."

The way she's looking at me makes my stomach drop. *Fuck.* Please don't let her be thinking about selling this place.

"What about it?" I ask tentatively with a glance at Amelia to make sure she's focused on her schoolwork.

"Let's sit down." She pours herself a Diet Coke and heads over to one of the tables.

I catch Amelia's eye. "You good?"

"Yep!" She smiles at me, and I'm filled with warmth. At least if Leena has bad news, I have a good thing going with Griffin and the kids. I sit across from Leena and wait for her to start.

"Bailey and I have been discussing plans for after the baby is born. We want to limit childcare as much as we can. Without having a mom myself, I really want to focus on spending as much time with the baby as possible."

I nod. I get where she's coming from, but my gut clenches with worry about where this is going.

"So, with all that said, I think I'll be stepping back a bit around here. What I was wondering is if you would have any interest in becoming a full partner instead of being the general manager."

I'm stunned and just blink at her for a few seconds. "What?"

"Honestly, it's how it should have been from the beginning. You go above and beyond for this place and do way more than your salary reflects." I start to argue with her, but she holds up a hand to stop me. "I know we've had this argument in the past, but I think this is the best solution. As a part owner, you'd make more from profit share, and you could make changes without needing to run everything by me. Obviously, give me a heads up if you want to knock down a wall or something, but I trust you to do what's best for the business."

"I don't know what to say. You'd really want me to be a part owner?"

"Of course! You love this place as much as I do. You should have been an owner from the beginning, but I had such tunnel vision of creating something completely mine. I'm not particularly concerned about the money side of your buying in. We could work something out in the profit-share ratios. Annie did a valuation for me so we could talk it all over with her."

"I have the money," I say quietly. "I'd want to buy in."

"You do?" she asks, surprised. I'm sure she's remembering when I was scrimping and saving for the down payment on my SUV.

"I, uh, my dad left me money when he died. A lot, actually. I had a financial guy put it into investment funds and accounts so it would grow, but I wasn't ready to do anything more with it. I'm not sure how much I've told you about my parents..."

"Almost nothing, Cass. You've always kept everything so close to your chest."

I clear my throat and nod. "I had a pretty rough childhood. From the outside, it probably looked perfect, but it wasn't behind closed doors. My mom is..." I blow out a big breath, about to tell someone my secrets for the first time in years. It's right that Leena knows. Meg and Zander are the only ones who are aware of the extent. "My mom is an abusive narcissist.

My dad wasn't abusive, but he didn't do much of anything to step in and protect me from her. They divorced when I was thirteen, and I was alone with her for five years. He and I weren't on the best of terms when he died because of it. So it's always felt weird to do anything with the money."

"Oh, Cass. I'm so sorry you had to go through so much shit as a kid. It honestly explains so much about you."

"Thanks," I deadpan.

"You know what I mean. It must be hard for you to trust people after what you've been through."

I swallow to keep down the emotion her words are bringing. "It is. It's also very hard for me to believe that other people can trust me. Love me."

"What do you mean?"

"I spent eighteen years with a mother who said really horrible things to me and about me, all the time. It's made it really hard to undo the things I've internalized."

"Oh my god. I'd really love to punch your mother. What a cunt." My eyes widen in shock. Leena's no stranger to curse words, but I know I've never heard her use that one. "I know, I hate the 'C' word, but I'm pretty sure it's the only one strong enough to describe your mother."

I huff a laugh. She's not wrong.

"You know I love you, right, Cass? Because I do. You've become a sister to me, just as much as Annie and Jessie."

Tears fill my eyes, and I nod my head. "I know. I love you, too." The words slip out, and I realize with a shock, I can't remember the last time I told someone I loved them. Probably with Meg or Zander, but I can't remember it.

"So, now we've gotten the emotional display over with," Leena says as she wipes tears from under her eyes, "can we go back to discussing becoming business partners?"

"Yes, I'm in. Let's do it."

Two hours and a visit with Annie later, we've got everything worked out for my transition from general manager of the Songbird to part owner. I have the paperwork to send over to my financial guy to look over, mostly because Annie insisted I should, ready to go.

Amelia joins in our celebratory toast, although both she and Leena have Sprite. "This is so fun. I'm glad I was here for this. You guys are friend goals," Amelia gushes as we sit back down. "Girl groups are badass, like Huntrix."

"Is that who you dressed up as for Halloween?" I ask, recognizing the name but having a hard time placing it.

"Yeah. *K-Pop Demon Hunters* is still huge."

"Because it's fucking awesome," Leena chimes in.

I shrug. "I never actually watched it."

All three of them stop and stare at me. "What do you mean you haven't watched it? Are you living under a rock?" Amelia shrieks at me.

"I know what it is. I've heard some of the songs, mostly here at open mic. I don't have Netflix, so I never really bothered."

"Come on, we're going home now. We have to fix this." She stands up and grabs her backpack.

I glance at my watch. We have about an hour until we usually head back to Griffin's house to meet him and Drew for dinner. I shrug and look at Leena.

"You guys go; Alaina will be here any minute to take over," she says, smiling. She grabs me and hugs me hard before we leave. I squeeze her back, thanking her wordlessly for everything that happened today.

"Alright, kid. Let's get out of here."

We leave the Songbird and head straight for Griffin's house. Amelia insists on popping popcorn and keeping the lights low so we get the full effect of the movie. I shake my head at her dramatics, but settle in to watch. I don't see a lot of newer movies, but she's so excited to watch this one with me.

How bad can it be?

Chapter Seventeen

Griffin

I'M SURPRISED TO SEE Cass and Amelia are already home when Drew and I get there. There's hardly any light on in the house, but Cass's car is out front. I flip the kitchen lights on as I walk through.

"Hello?" I call out.

"In here!" Amelia calls out from the family room. Between the smell of popcorn and the flicker of the TV, they must be watching a movie.

I pop into the room to find Amelia and Cass snuggled up at opposite ends of the couch. *K-Pop Demon Hunters* plays on the large TV. I plop myself down on the center cushion between them. "We haven't done this one in a while. I thought you were burnt out on it?" I ask.

"Cass has never seen it," Amelia responds.

"What? How is that possible?"

Cass groans and tips her head back against the couch. "I don't have Netflix. I just never bothered tracking it down."

I reach out and squeeze her calf, and she shoots me a smile before her attention goes back to the screen. We all chuckle when the main girl jump-scares the demon guy. At some point in the movie, Drew wanders in and curls up in the armchair. I revel in how perfect it feels to be watching a movie with Cass and the kids, like we're already a solid family unit.

I could see this being a normal night. A random movie on the TV and my favorite people around me. I want it so much it makes my whole body ache with longing. I get comfortable and settle in to watch with them.

Cass is incredibly focused on the movie, almost like she's entranced. I catch her watching with a furrowed brow multiple times, although she laughs out loud at the tiger's antics. She steals glances at me during the song "Free," and I wonder for the hundredth time what she's thinking.

She's visibly upset when shit hits the fan in the movie, and I squeeze her leg again. I'm getting concerned about how Cass is taking this movie. When the main girl confronts the woman who raised her, a slow trickle of tears starts down Cass's face. She tries to hide them, but I see them. They don't stop throughout the rest of the movie.

When the end credits roll and Amelia excitedly looks over at Cass and asks what she thought, Cass breaks, a choked sob escaping her. Amelia's eyes go wide, and Drew looks scared.

"Guys, I think Cass needs a minute. Why don't you go see what leftovers we can heat up for dinner?"

"Okay, Daddy. Come on, Drew." They hustle out of the room, throwing back concerned looks as they leave.

I scoop Cass up so she's sitting sideways on my lap and wrap my arms around her. She melts into me and sobs into my chest. Clearly, something about the movie broke down the armor she keeps so tightly locked around herself. I don't know whether to be relieved or terrified.

When she's calmed down a bit, I finally ask, "You want to talk about it?"

"I'm sorry." She sits up and scrubs at the tears covering her face. "I don't know what just happened."

"There's nothing for you to be sorry about. Are you all right?"

She nods. "The movie just hit some sore spots for me, I guess." She stands up, shaking off the emotion of the last twenty minutes. I can almost see her armor slipping back into place. "Should we see what the kids were able to find for dinner?"

"Cass, it's okay to talk about whatever affected you about the movie."

She shakes her head tightly. "I'm okay, really."

I nod, and she makes a quick exit from the room, claiming she needs the restroom. I follow her out, but I can't shake the worry taking up residence in my gut. She's quiet and withdrawn throughout dinner, and I almost expect her to leave for the night, but surprisingly, she doesn't.

When we're in bed for the night, she curls her body around mine and holds on tight like she's trying to hold herself together. I have some suspicions that the movie shook loose some feelings about her childhood, and now she's doing her best to bottle them back up.

I just hope she'll let me pick up the pieces when the bottle finally bursts.

A WEEK AFTER THE movie incident, I come home from a day in the office to the sound of piano music floating from the family room. I don't own a piano, so I'm automatically confused, but since Cass was bringing the kids home today, I'm sure she has something to do with it.

Before I can make it to the room, Cass and Drew's voices join the piano, singing together. I recognize "Giants in the Sky" from *Into the Woods* thanks to Drew's obsession with the show, and smile at the way they sing together before the song stops.

"Good, okay, you try it on your own," Cass says softly. Drew sings the same line of the song by himself. "Really good!" I'm not sure I've ever heard Cass speak with such warmth and softness, so I hesitate outside the room to listen in.

My heart melts as I stand and listen to Cass coach Drew on the song for a few more minutes before I make my way into the room. Cass has a portable keyboard similar to what they use at the Songbird set up in the middle of the family room. She's seated at the piano with her iPad resting on the music stand. I take a seat on the couch and smile at them, prompting a pause in their practice.

"Dad! I'm gonna audition for *Into the Woods*!"

"If your parents say it's okay," Cass qualifies. She looks up at me and smiles. "I saw the audition notice while I was scrolling Insta today. They're doing the Jr. version at the Starling Company, and I may have mentioned it to him prematurely."

"Sounds like fun, buddy."

"I'll send you the audition info so you can make sure the rehearsal schedule works," Cass says kind of nervously.

"I'm sure we can make it happen," I assure them both. "Let me hear the song again."

Drew grins and bounces on his toes, and Cass shoots me a full, beautiful smile. She might be just as excited about this as Drew is. I will be making sure this audition happens no matter what.

Drew sings the part full out, and while I may be biased, he sounds damn good. When they're done, I clap my hands loudly, and Drew takes an exaggerated bow, making Cass and me laugh.

"Dad, Cass can do the whole part the witch does in the opening. Cass, show him."

"Your dad has heard me sing plenty at open mic nights, kiddo."

"I wouldn't mind a repeat performance." I grin at her, daring her to turn us down. Amelia wanders in and plops into the armchair across the room.

"What are you guys doing?" she asks, looking back and forth between Cass and me.

"Cass was gonna sing something for us," I say boldly, raising my eyebrows in challenge.

Cass groans. "Fine. What should I sing?"

"What about that song you were working on the other day at the café? It sounded so good," Amelia suggests. Cass stares at the piano keys for a hot second before she nods and taps a few times on her iPad. She clears her throat and starts singing softly.

I don't recognize the song, but it's a gorgeous melody that works perfectly with Cass's voice. It's clear watching her that Cass chose to work on this song for a reason, so I close my eyes and focus on the lyrics she's singing. It's a song about following her heart and making her own choices to live her best life. I can't help but hope she's talking about choosing our family.

When she's done, the last note echoes in the room for a beat before the kids, and I applaud. Cass gives us a shy smile as she turns off the keyboard. She stands and comes to sit next to me on the couch.

"Happy now?"

"Very," I say as I loop my arm around her shoulders. She leans her head back against me, snuggling in, and I'm not sure I could be happier than I am right now in this moment. "What was the song?"

"It's called 'My Days' from *The Notebook* musical. I've been toying with it the last couple of weeks."

"I love it," Amelia says in a reverent tone, smiling at Cass.

"What's for dinner?" Drew pipes up, in typically nine-year-old boy fashion. "Can we have Puerto Rican food again?"

"I don't think we have all the ingredients for it tonight, kiddo, but we can make it soon," Cass answers, smiling.

"I was thinking we could order pizzas. What do you think?"

Drew pumps his fist. "Yes! Can I play my Switch until it gets here?"

"Sure, bud."

Amelia mumbles something about texting her friends and follows Drew out of the room. I turn to ask Cass what she wants for pizza toppings, to find her staring into space, an anxious look on her face.

"Cass?" I say her name softly, and she doesn't seem to hear me until I've repeated it louder. She snaps her gaze to me then.

She gives me a sheepish smile. "Sorry, what was that?"

"You okay?" I ask, officially concerned at the faraway look in her eye.

"Of course." She smiles, but it doesn't quite reach her eyes. This has happened a couple of times since she was so affected by *K-Pop Demon Hunters*, and I wish she would tell me what she's thinking about when she zones out like that. I'm dying for her to let me in, but it's not like I can force her, so I do my best to make sure she knows I'm here for her.

She's gotta let me in at some point.

Right?

A COUPLE OF WEEKS pass by without incident, but every so often, Cass seems to fold in on herself, usually when she thinks no one's looking. I've tried to ask her what's wrong, to get her to open up. She insists she's fine, but her zoning out is happening more often, and each time it happens, dread fills my stomach.

Which is why when I pull into my driveway to find Leena's car instead of Cass's, I know right away something is wrong in my house. I park in the garage and hustle into the house as fast as I can. I find Leena in the kitchen, pulling some sort of casserole out of the oven.

"Hey, Griffin. Dinner is just about done." She gives me a pained smile.

"What's going on? Where are the kids? Where's Cass?" I ask immediately.

She sighs and turns off the oven. "First, everyone is safe. Both of the kids are in their rooms finishing homework."

"Cass?"

Leena cringes. "She needs some time."

"What the fuck happened, Leena?" I demand, panic setting in.

Leena sags, placing a hand on her small baby bump. "Let's sit down, and I'll tell you what I know."

I blow out a shaky breath as I pull out a kitchen chair for Leena and take a seat myself.

"Spill, Leens." I grit out.

"Okay. About two hours ago, I got a call from Cass, asking me to come hang out with the kids until you got home. She sounded so freaked out, I came straight over. The only thing she would tell me was she 'thought she could do this, but she's not cut out for it.' She's headed to Beachville Springs to spend some time with her friend Meg for a while."

"Not cut out for what?"

"She wouldn't clarify for me, but I'm gonna guess she meant being around the kids."

"Fuck. So she just left? What the fuck happened here?" I drag my hands through my hair. What could have possibly happened to make Cass run like this?

"From what I got out of Amelia, Cass had a very rough phone call with her mother this afternoon. She said it put Cass in a bad mood. Drew happened to be chattering about something on Minecraft, and Cass apparently snapped at him. Drew got upset and ran to his room. Amelia then said something very teenager-y and stormed off herself. I think that's about when Cass called me. Amelia was very upset when she came back out and found Cass gone."

"Jesus Christ. What a mess. What do I do here, Leena? Do I try to go after Cass?"

"No. How much do you know about Cass's mother?"

"Almost nothing. I got the idea from Amelia that Cass had a rough childhood, but she's never told me anything directly. What am I missing here?"

Leena frowns. "She didn't give me any specific details, but she called her mother 'an abusive narcissist,' so I can't imagine the phone call was good. I'm pretty sure she's been no-contact with her mom since her dad died. So, hearing from her out of the blue..." The hairs on the back of my neck stand on end. It's a piece of the puzzle of Cass that I didn't have before. Leena reaches over and squeezes my hand. "She was visibly upset about what happened with the kids. I think she needs some time with Meg to reset and work through it."

"What if... What if she doesn't come back?" I say, my voice barely above a whisper.

"She'll at least come back for the Songbird. We already signed all the paperwork to become a part owner."

"What if she doesn't come back to me? To us? *Fuck.* I practically had to beg her to be in this relationship. What if she's done?"

Leena clenches her jaw and stares at the tabletop. "Honestly, it's a possibility. Cass has a lot of practice in being closed off and pushing people away. But... I think she really cares about you and the kids. This is the happiest I've ever seen her. I'm hoping she works through this instead of going backward." I run my hands over my face, and Leena stands up. "Take care of the kids, Griff, and don't lose hope."

"Thanks, Leena."

She pats me on the back one more time before letting herself out the front door. I cover my face with my hands and rest my elbows on the table. How did everything fall apart so quickly?

"Daddy?" A soft voice calls out from the entrance to the kitchen.

I look up to find a distraught-looking Amelia standing looking at me.

"Hey, sweetie. You hungry? Aunt Leena left dinner for us." I try to make my voice sound as normal as possible, but I don't succeed.

"Daddy, I'm sorry." Amelia whines, tears sliding down her face.

"Oh, Amelia. None of this is your fault."

"I said she was being a bitch. I could tell she was upset, but I still said it. It's all my fault."

"Baby girl. It's alright. Come here." I wrap her in my arms and pull her into the family room so we can sit on the couch. "Cass did not leave because of what you said. She has some things she needs to work through, and I think she didn't want to upset you and Drew more, so she called Aunt Leena in."

"With her mom?" Mellie asks, and the hairs stand up on my neck again. "I couldn't hear her whole phone call, but you should have seen her face when she answered the phone. It was almost like she was scared of who was calling, but then she called her 'Mother' and went into the bathroom. I heard Cass yelling at one point. I could tell she was upset when she came out, but she pretended not to be until Drew wouldn't shut up about making his Minecraft world look like Neverland. I was gonna tell him to shut up, but Cass did first, and then he cried, and she looked scared again. I freaked out and asked her why she was being a bitch, and ran to my room. I'm sorry, Daddy."

Amelia sobs into my chest, and I rub her back. My heart breaks for all three of them. Clearly, Cass hit her breaking point from the phone call, and I wasn't here. She told me she didn't want to be a mom, but here she was, taking care of my kids, just like she's done for weeks. *Fuck.*

Drew comes out of his room, and I have to start the reassurance all over again. I make sure they know it was not their fault. Sometimes, grown-ups lose their tempers when they're having a bad day, and Cass was leaving to figure some things out. I do my best to be vague about when we'll see her again, because what if she wants nothing to do with us?

Once I've gotten them both fed and in bed for the night, I sit on the edge of my bed with a glass of scotch. I try calling Cass, but unsurprisingly, she doesn't answer. I decide to text her instead.

Me:

> **I want you to know I'm not mad about what went down today. I don't love how you left, but I understand you needed space.**

I give it a few minutes, but there's no response.

Me:

> **The kids are okay. Every parent in the history of the world has snapped at their kids, and they're resilient.**

A few more minutes pass without an answer.

Me:

> **I'm sorry if I put too much pressure on you. I care about you, Cass. So much. Please just let me know you're alright.**

Me:

Spitfire, please.

Clearly not getting an answer tonight, I slam back my glass and get ready for bed. I spend the night tossing and turning, wondering if Cass has spent her last night in my bed and beating myself up for not making sure she knows how much I love her.

Chapter Eighteen

Cass

"CAN YOU SHUT UP *for like two seconds? Why do you feel the need to be talking all the time?"*

The words echo in my mind, even in my sleep. In my head, it's not my voice, like it was with Drew yesterday. No, it's my mother's voice. It's something I heard her say to me more times than I can count.

I sit up in bed, disoriented. *Where the fuck am I?* Oh, right. I'm in Meg's guest bedroom because I ran when my mother's voice came out of my mouth with Drew and Amelia. I check my phone to find a series of text messages from Griffin.

Shit.

Even after everything, he's being so sweet and understanding. Doesn't he realize I became my mother yesterday, and his children were caught in the crossfire? This is exactly why I never wanted to be a mom. I refuse to hurt Amelia and Drew the way I was hurt.

I read the messages but click away from the thread without responding, just as a light knock sounds on the bedroom door. Meg doesn't wait for me to respond before coming in with two mugs of coffee and a cautious look on her face.

"How are you feeling this morning?" she asks as she hands me the coffee.

"Like shit. Thanks for letting me crash."

"Of course. Are you ready to tell me what the fuck happened? I let you wallow and hide last night, but now it's time to talk it out, babes."

I sigh, knowing she won't let it go. "My mom called yesterday."

Her eyes go wide. "I thought you blocked her."

"I did. She used her new fiancé's phone."

"What the fuck?"

"Apparently, she had been trying to contact me, and she finally realized I must have her blocked, so she tried calling from a different number," I explain, pinching the bridge of my nose to hold back the emotions still lingering at the surface.

"What did she want?"

I think back to the awful call and hearing my mother's voice for the first time in almost five years.

"HELLO?"

"Cassidee. Finally. I've been trying to contact you for weeks."

"Mother."

All the blood drains from my face. I motion to Amelia that I have to take the call, and I lock myself in the hall bathroom at Griffin's house. I should have hung up right there.

"What do you want?"

"Really nice. This is how you'll talk to the person who gave you life?"

I take a deep breath and try not to engage with her. "What do you want, Mom?"

"Well, I've been calling to tell you. I'm getting remarried next month. Tim keeps asking if you'll be joining us. You need to come to the wedding."

"There's not a chance in hell of my coming to your wedding," I grit out.

"Don't be ridiculous. You're my only daughter; you should be here. It would mean so much to me."

"What you mean is Tim hasn't realized what a narcissist you are, and you don't want to explain why your only daughter wants nothing to do with you."

"I can't believe you would say such hurtful things to me. I gave up everything to give you life. I did everything to raise you right, and you've become such a disappointment. Your father would be ashamed to see you now."

"Don't you dare talk about Daddy to me." I try hard to keep my voice down, but she knows exactly how to push my buttons.

"This is exactly why you haven't settled down. Who would love someone so combative and ungrateful? I don't know where I went wrong with you."

"Maybe it was all the times you slapped me for talking too much or not getting good enough grades. Or cut my calories so strictly, I threw up from my stomach being empty." I grit out, fighting tears as the memories flood me.

She gasps as if my words are shocking. "Oh, I did no such thing. You're such a liar. You know what? I don't want you at my wedding; you'll just come and spread lies about me. Goodbye, Cassidee. I hope if you ever have children, they're just like you, so you can see what you really put me through."

And just like that, she was gone, leaving me a broken mess, just like she had every day for eighteen years.

I SNAP BACK TO the present to find Meg staring at me, concerned. I try to explain, but no words come out, just a deep, wracking sob. Meg pulls me against her and hugs me for what seems like an hour until my breath comes easier.

Eventually, I'm able to tell her how everything happened with the kids after the phone call from hell, and I show her the texts from Griffin that I still haven't answered.

"How is he not furious with me?" I ask her, confused.

"Because literally every parent ever has snapped at their kid at some point. We're human." She shrugs like it's no big deal, and maybe for people like Meg and Griffin, it isn't. But the second my mother's words came launching out of my mouth at Drew, something clicked into place.

I am not fit to be anyone's mom. Not even a stepmom. It's too much responsibility, and I refuse to be the one who breaks those amazing kids.

I shake my head. "I'm not cut out for parenthood. It's better we found out now, before we all became too attached." My voice breaks on the last word, because I know it's too late. I'm attached to all of them, and stepping away is going to hurt like a motherfucker. But I have to do what's best for the kids. What's best for Griffin.

I only hope someday he'll understand.

MEG AND I SPEND most of the day hashing and rehashing everything that happened. One of her brothers-in-law picks up Beckett for us so that we can split a couple of bottles of wine without worrying about him.

I still think breaking things off is the inevitable right choice, but Meg insisted I have a session with my long-term therapist before I make any permanent decisions. She stole my phone to keep me from texting Griffin to break things off. Together, we craft a text to him that assures him that I'm safe and need some space, but she doesn't let me do the typing.

The next day I spend almost the whole day playing with Beckett, which makes me feel a little better. When I ask Meg for my phone, she hands it over, but she watches me like a hawk. Griffin, of course, texted to tell me that he'd be there when I'm ready to talk. He can't make it easy and be pissed at me. I can't bring myself to respond, so I give my phone back to Meg so I don't have to look at it.

My phone is back in my possession when it's time for my video call with Linda on Saturday morning. It's been over a year since we last spoke, but she's been my therapist for almost ten years. I first met her at the school's counseling center when I was struggling in my sophomore year of college. When she moved to telehealth a few years ago, I followed her.

Linda is a tiny blonde woman, probably in her mid-fifties. Her golden hair is tightly curled, and she wears glasses in fun, bold colors; purple today. She gives me a warm smile through the screen.

"Cass! It's so good to see you! It's been a while."

I try to smile back. It doesn't go well. "Hi, Linda. Thanks for fitting me in on a Saturday."

Her smile turns sad. "I take it this isn't a random session to catch up. Why don't you fill me in?"

I tell her everything. I describe what my life looked like before meeting Griffin. I go through every step of our relationship, from our hidden identity one-night stand to practically becoming a part of his family. She nods along, asking questions here and there to clarify things.

Then, I get into the call with my mother. She knows all about my history with her and was one of the biggest champions of my going no-contact after my dad died. Finally, I tell her about how I lashed out at Drew.

"You should have seen his face. He was so upset, and he ran to his room crying. And then Amelia asked why I was being such a bitch. I swear, I was transported back to being her age and thinking the same thing about my mom. After everything, I became her anyway."

"Now wait a minute here. Why would you say you became your mom?"

"I literally said the exact thing she used to say to me. This is exactly why I never wanted to become a mom. We talked about this when I decided to have my tubes removed. We both know I'm not fit to be a mom."

"Hey, now. Don't put words in my mouth. I agreed you had the right to choose not to be a mother. I never said you weren't fit for it. If anything, I think you'd be a rather wonderful mom."

"Have you been listening? What I said to Drew was awful. Even Amelia, who up until this point has been my biggest fan, thinks I'm a bitch. It's best for them both if I step away."

"Alright. Let's slow down and unpack this. What you said to Drew wasn't great, but all parents lose their cool. Spending non-stop time with kids is stressful. The biggest factor here is how you reacted after. How you felt."

"Okay..." I scrunch my nose and think. "I felt like a terrible person who shouldn't be around kids."

"Were you sorry for hurting his feelings?"

"Of course. I'll never forget his devastated little face."

"Do you think your mom felt bad when she said the same thing to you?" Huh. She's got me there. "When you confronted your mom on the phone the other day, did she own up to the things she'd done? Did she apologize?"

"Of course not. She claimed I was lying."

"Exactly. What would you say to Drew and Amelia if they were with you right now? Would you claim they were lying about what happened?"

"Okay. I see your point. I would apologize, making sure they all knew how sorry I was for lashing out."

"I need you to really hear me on this one, Cass. You are not your mother. Not even close. You're the one who gets to decide to break the cycle of abuse." She lets the words hang in the air for a beat. "Now, if you really don't *want* to be in a parenting role, then by all means, walk away from the relationship. But if there's a chance that being with Griffin and joining his family is what you want for your future, don't let this be one more thing your mother ruins for you."

We talk some more about handling negative self-talk and not letting the lies my mother beat into my head for years become my truth. We decide it's best for me to return to regular sessions with Linda while I'm navigating all of this, so we schedule another call for next week.

When I hang up the call with Linda, I flop back onto the bed and blow out a huge breath. Everything she said made so much sense, but can I really just go back?

After a few minutes of thinking myself in circles, I realize I can hear voices whispering on the other side of the door. They're fighting about whether they should check on me, and I chuckle to myself.

"You guys can come in!" I yell out, and the voices stop.

The door bursts open, and Zander comes racing in. He takes a running jump onto the bed and wraps me in his arms. I snuggle into him, taking comfort in his strong arms, even if they're not exactly the arms I want to be wrapped in. They'll work for now.

"My poor Dee Dee," he murmurs and drops a smacking kiss to my forehead.

"Don't call me that," I grumble.

"Glad to see your grumpy attitude is surviving this time of hardship. Now. Meggy filled me in on the drama with your Jonathan Bailey-looking stud and his munchkins, but what I want to know is what you're going to do about it."

I laugh and shake my head as Meg steps into the room with a tray full of tiny bowls of ice cream toppings and three pints of ice cream. We all get comfortable at the head of the bed and get situated with our ice cream feast before I tell them the fears that have been plaguing me since I got off the phone with Linda.

"What if he doesn't want me anymore?"

Zander and Meg both scoff at me. "There's no chance. Didn't he basically text you a novel to tell you he wasn't mad?" he asks before shoving a huge spoonful of ice cream in his beautiful face.

"Well, yeah. But I barely texted him back. I told him I was okay, but I needed space. That was two days ago. What if he's given up on me by now?"

I get another eye roll from the two of them. "With everything you know about this man, do you really believe he'd give up on you so easily?" Meg asks.

I sigh. "No... I'm just scared."

"Putting yourself out there, really putting your heart on the line, is scary as fuck. And there's a chance you could get hurt. You could break up, or one of you could die unexpectedly." I link my arm through Meg's arm and squeeze. Her eyes fill with tears. She's come such a long way since Gavin died, but I know she still has hard days. "All I'm saying is, loving people as fully as you can is always worth it."

"Does that mean you're ready to get back out there and start dating?" Zander asks her. Meg rolls her eyes and stabs her spoon into her pint of ice cream.

"I've actually been thinking about that lately."

My eyes widen, and I meet Zander's equally surprised expression. We didn't see that coming.

"Oh my god, Meggy. Did you meet someone?" Zander squeals.

"No. No, I'm just...open to the idea of someone."

"Well, holy shit," I murmur, taking another big bite of cookie dough ice cream.

"Holy shit indeed. Cassidee, if our lovely Meggy can be entertaining the idea of dating again, I think you can certainly handle winning back Griffin."

I blow out a big breath and lean my head on Meg's shoulder. "You guys are right. I have to try. I just... I have to figure out how. I feel like it needs to be bigger than just showing up at his house and begging him to love me."

"I'm convinced this man already loves you. He probably was afraid of you freaking out and running away if he told you. Oh wait... You did it anyway," Zander says in a snarky tone.

"Fuck off!" I punch him playfully in the arm. He laughs and blows me a kiss. "I love you guys. I don't say it enough, but I do."

"We love you too, Dee Dee," Meg says with a kiss to the top of my head. "We always will."

I snuggle in with my two best friends in the world. Being with them used to be my favorite place in the world, but somewhere along the way, things changed.

Now, my favorite place is wherever Griffin and the kids are. I just hope they'll take me back.

Chapter Nineteen

Griffin

IT'S BEEN TWO DAYS since I heard from Cass, and I'm crawling out of my skin with anxiety. The text she sent on Thursday wasn't particularly reassuring. I guess it was better than nothing, though. We've come too far for her to ghost me at this point.

I hope.

Luckily, it's Nessa's weekend, and I can continue to stew in my misery alone. I thought about going to the Songbird for a drink, but I didn't think I could stand being there without Cass. Or worse, what if I found her there behind the bar, acting as if nothing happened?

When the doorbell rings in the late afternoon, my heart leaps into my throat. Maybe Cass wanted to talk in person, and that's why she hasn't texted me again. I yank the front door open, and my heart drops to find Dan and Eric on the front step. My whole body slumps, and I run a hand through my hair.

"Hey, guys. What are you doing here?"

"Wow, what a warm welcome," Eric deadpans with a smirk. Dan chuckles next to him, holding up a couple of six-packs of beer.

"Bailey had a photoshoot in New York for one of his sponsorships, but he and Leena thought you could use some company," Dan explains.

I sigh and step back to let them in. I lead them into the family room and collapse into one corner of the couch. Dan hands me an open beer and grabs the remote from the end table. I take a long drink from the bottle before I ask, "I take it Leena filled you in on everything that went down this week?"

"Yup. Have you heard from Cass?" Eric asks as he sits at the other end of the couch. Dan flips through the TV channels before landing on an old Flash game before sitting in the armchair.

"She texted on Thursday to say she needed space. Haven't heard from her since." They both wince. "Has Leena heard from her?"

Dan shakes his head. "I don't think she's heard any more than you, and she said Cass hasn't come back to the Songbird yet. I'm sure Cass will reach out when she's ready."

I blow out a big breath, a little relieved at the knowledge that Cass is still in Beachville Springs, and try to focus on my brother pitching on the TV. Without looking at either of them, I voice the fears that have consumed me since Cass took off. "What if she doesn't?"

When I risk a glance at Dan and Eric, I can see they're having some kind of telepathic conversation. They nod at each other, having decided something, and Dan takes the lead.

"You know we've known Cass a long time, right?" I nod and gesture for Dan to continue. "I met her for the first time during her freshman year of college. I didn't get to know her well. I don't think she and Jessie vibed, but she bonded with Leena. Cass has been on the outskirts of our friend group for the last thirteen years, and I don't remember seeing her smile as much in all those years combined as she has these last few months with you."

"We've all seen the change in her." Eric chimes in. "I mean, she's still pretty standoffish and low-key scary, but there's something more relaxed about her."

I chuckle, knowing exactly what he means. I know they're right. Cass has been happier since we got together. But is it enough?

"I think she'll come around. Leena hinted that Cass had a rough childhood, and I can tell you parent issues can cause freak outs when relationships start to get serious," Eric says.

My eyebrows raise at that. "You or Annie?"

He huffs a laugh. "A little bit of both. I freaked out on her in college. She tried to run from me when we finally got together last year." He shrugs. "We both have daddy issues that took some therapy to work through."

I nod and stare at the TV some more. "I wish she knew how much I love her. I haven't said it because I was afraid of freaking her out, but now I wish she knew."

Dan laughs this time. "She knows. Anyone who's looked at you in the last couple of months knows."

"And for the record, you can't convince me that she doesn't love you," Eric adds. I open my mouth to respond, but nothing comes out. "Now, should we order some food and re-watch Bailey strike out most of Chicago's lineup?"

We order food and watch the game, but my mind doesn't leave Eric's declaration. I spend the evening hoping with every fiber of my being that he's right.

WHEN NESSA DROPS THE kids off the next afternoon, she takes one look at me and pulls me into a hug. I take a moment of comfort and hold on to her, even if she's not the woman I really need to be holding in my arms.

When she pulls back, she gives me a sympathetic smile. "Amelia filled me in on what happened. Have you heard from her?"

I shake my head. "Not for a few days. Want to stay for a cup of coffee? I could use the feminine perspective on the situation."

Nessa laughs and follows me into the kitchen. Thanks to sleeping like shit every night since Cass has been gone, I had already made a fresh pot of coffee. I pour the coffee, adding a ton of cream and sugar to Nessa's cup and significantly less to mine.

I give Nessa a quick rundown of the text Cass sent and what little I know of Cass's childhood via Leena. Nessa stares into her coffee with a furrowed brow.

"Well?"

"I'd like to pick Cass's brain about Girls on the Run. She said it helped her as a kid. I wonder if she'd join the board."

"Nessa! Can you focus on my situation here?"

Nessa chuckles and waves me off. "She'll be back. She'd be crazy to walk away from you."

I raise my eyebrows and cross my arms over my chest. "Nessa. You walked away from me."

Nessa rolls her eyes and smiles. "Seriously, Griff. You and I never had what you and Cass do. The chemistry between you can be felt from across the room. She's not leaving you."

"I hope you're right."

"You should know by now, I'm always right." She finishes her coffee and starts to stand from her seat at my kitchen table, but I stop her with a hand on her elbow.

"I've always wondered. Was there... someone? Someone you had chemistry with?"

Nessa swallows hard and fiddles with the coffee mug. "Nothing happened."

"That's not what I asked, Ness."

She blows a big puff of air through her lips. "Yeah. There was... someone. But he was engaged, and I was married. He was only working with the company short-term, a financial consultant. We had... a moment, but nothing happened. He left shortly after, and I never heard from him again."

"But it changed things?"

Nessa sighs and nods. "Yeah. I tried to forget about it for close to six months, but I couldn't. I'm sorry I didn't tell you."

I grab Nessa's hand. "It's okay. I suspected that *something* must have happened for you to suddenly want a divorce. And you were right about it being for the best. So you never reached out to him?"

"No. He was engaged and left... abruptly. I don't think he'd want to hear from me." She gives me a sad smile. "I'm just happy to know that kind of spark exists, even if I'm a little jealous you found it first."

We both laugh, and it feels good to stop wallowing in my fear about Cass for a few minutes. After Nessa leaves, I stand in the pantry trying to figure out dinner when Drew comes in.

"Hey buddy, did you have fun with Mom this weekend?"

"Yeah. She listened to my audition song a bunch of times. She found the song on her phone since she can't play piano like Cass."

"Well, that's good," I say, ignoring the pang in my chest at Cass's name. "What do you want for dinner?"

"Can we have Puerto Rican food? We still haven't had it again, and it sounds good."

I blow out a long breath. "Drew, I don't know how to make that. Plus, I don't think we have the ingredients. I don't even know what goes in it."

"Oh. Can you text Cass and ask her?" Drew asks, his face scrunched in confusion.

"I think she's still out of town, kiddo. I don't want to bother her while she's spending time with her friend."

Amelia comes in while I'm talking and crosses her arms. "When *is* Cass coming back?"

I bite the inside of my cheek. "I'm not sure, sweetie."

Amelia studies me. Her eyes get glassy, and her angry expression morphs into pure despair. "Did she break up with you? Does she not like us anymore?"

Fuck.

"Cass loves you guys. Right now, she's taking some time to spend with her friend Meg. I'm sure she'll come back soon."

"But you don't know. She might break up with you because of us."

I pinch the bridge of my nose. It was bad enough to think these things to myself. It's so much worse hearing the sentiment coming from my thirteen-year-old, her voice laced with fear and anger.

"I've always tried to be honest with you guys. There's a chance that things might not work between Cass and me. She's visiting Meg, and we'll talk when she comes back. But no matter what happens, it will not be your fault if Cass and I decide to go back to being friends."

The words feel bitter on my tongue, and Amelia scowls like she knows just how much I'd hate to be just friends with Cass. I slap a fake smile on my face that only makes both kids frown harder.

"Now, what should we have for dinner?"

Luckily, Amelia decides to take mercy on me and suggests, "Pancakes? Do we have other stuff for breakfast for dinner?"

"Yes!" Drew exclaims, the tension of the last few minutes forgotten. Amelia gives me a sad smile as she pulls bacon and eggs out of the fridge.

"Perfect." I agree and get started making the pancake batter. I do my best to shake away the bad mood, but I notice Amelia studying me with a sad look more than once.

I'm not the only one who misses Cass, and I'm not the only one who will be hurt if she decides to be done with our relationship. I vow to myself to do everything I possibly can to convince Cass she belongs here. She has already become part of our family.

We need her to stay.

Chapter Twenty

Cass

AFTER HIDING OUT AT Meg's house for the weekend, I finally snuck home late Sunday night, knowing the bar would be closed. I wanted just one night to get myself together before facing everyone here.

Mid-morning on Monday, I pop out into the bar after another shitty night of sleep to find Amelia sitting at the bar with a smoothie, talking to Leena. I freeze in my tracks, not realizing I'd be facing her first thing in the morning. Why isn't she at school?

"Cass!" Amelia cries out before rushing around the bar to me. She wraps her skinny arms around my waist, and I can't stop the tears from leaking out of my eyes.

"Hey, kid. Why aren't you in school?" I ask softly, squeezing her back and resting my chin on the top of her head.

"Teacher in-service. Aunt Leena said I could hang out here instead of staying home with Dad." She pulls back to look up at me, her huge hazel eyes sad. "I'm sorry I called you a bitch."

I chuckle. "It's alright, kid. I was being kind of a bitch. You know it had nothing to do with you or Drew, right?"

She nods her head. "My dad said sometimes grown-ups have a bad day and say things they don't mean. I do it too sometimes."

Christ. This man. He might actually be perfect. "He's exactly right, but I'm still sorry I took it out on you guys."

"Was it because you talked to your mom?" Amelia asks as she makes her way around the bar back to her seat.

I sigh. "Yes. My mom is not a nice person, and talking to her hurts me. It's part of why I'm not sure I have what it takes to be a mom. You and your brother deserve to have the best people in your lives taking care of you."

Amelia studies me for a minute. "I don't need a mom."

I furrow my brow, wondering where she's going with this. "What?"

"I don't need a mom. I already have one, and thanks to you, I know she's a pretty good one." I smile at her, glad she's finally giving Nessa the credit she deserves. Before I can comment, she continues, "I don't need a mom, but I do think I need you. I think we all do. Please don't leave us again."

This time, I'm the one hustling around the bar to wrap her up in a hug. Leena, who had stepped away to give us a moment to talk, comes back out to find us still hugging when she comes out from the kitchen with some clean glasses. She smiles at us, tears in her eyes.

"Fuck these pregnancy hormones," Leena says gruffly, swiping at her eyes. "I didn't even hear your conversation, and I'm crying just looking at you guys." Amelia and I both laugh.

We look up as the door opens and Nessa walks in.

"Hi Mom!" Amelia chirps, moving back onto her seat. "Do we have to leave right away?"

"Nope, I was just coming by to see if you wanted to grab lunch while your brother is still at his theater program. We can hang out here for a bit, or even order lunch to be delivered here." She smiles and looks up at me, standing next to Amelia's chair. "Cass, it's good to see you back."

I swallow hard. It's obvious she knows about everything that happened. Griffin would never keep that kind of information from her. *Fuck.* What if she doesn't want me around the kids anymore? I was so worried about winning Griffin's forgiveness, but I need Nessa's, too.

As if she's reading my mind, Nessa asks, "Cass, do you think we could have a quick chat?" I tilt my head toward the kitchen area, and she nods. "Amelia, figure out where you want lunch from while I talk to Cass."

"Okay, Mom."

I lead Nessa up to my apartment and offer her a bottle of water from my fridge. We sit at the tiny kitchen table.

"Nessa, I'm so sorry. You trusted me with your children, and I totally fucked it up."

"Cass. That's not why I wanted to talk to you." She smiles and reaches out to squeeze my hand. I stare at her, confused. "I'm glad you're making things right with Griff and the kids, but you don't owe me an apology."

"I really think I do," I stammer out. "I want you to trust me with Amelia and Drew."

"Cass, losing your temper once does not outweigh the positive effects you've had on the kids and Griffin, over the last few months. Honestly, it's a rite of passage, welcome to parenthood."

"I never planned to be a parent," I grumble.

Nessa laughs. "Shouldn't have fallen for a man with kids then."

"Trust me, I tried not to." We laugh together for a moment before I remember there was another reason she wanted to talk. "If you didn't want to talk about what happened…"

"Oh shit, yes. I wanted to gauge your interest in joining the board for Girls on the Run. Leena hinted a bit about your childhood, which you absolutely do not need to share with me, but I thought, as a former GOTR girl, your perspective could be helpful."

"Aren't board members usually, I don't know, super successful people?"

Nessa's eyebrows shoot up. "Cass, you have an MBA and are a small business owner. You are a successful person."

My mouth gapes open for a second before I snap it shut. I shake my head. "We'll just add that to the list of things to discuss with my therapist next week."

Nessa laughs and stands. "Think about joining us. We'd love to have your insight. Now let's go see what Amelia wants for lunch."

We leave my apartment together, and it's amazing how much lighter I already feel. I can only hope my conversations with Drew and Griffin go half as well.

Nessa perches on a barstool next to Amelia, scrolling through a food delivery app for lunch options, and I slide onto the stool on Amelia's other side. She shoots me a sparkling grin, and I'm not sure how I got lucky enough to be a part of her life.

"So, Cass, what's the plan?" Leena asks as she sets a coffee in front of me.

"What are you talking about?"

"Your plan to grand gesture Griffin? I mean, I guess you can just go talk it out, but that feels pretty anticlimactic, don't you think?" Leena hits me with a wolfish smile. "I'm sorry I haven't been documenting you as you slowly fell in love with him in a series of videos that I strategically send to him when you fucked up."

I roll my eyes at her recount of exactly what I did during her early days with Bailey. "Hey! Those videos worked!"

She chuckles. "They did. And now it's your turn to get *your* Turner brother locked down. Any ideas?"

Amelia raises her hand. "I have an idea!"

We both turn to look at the devious look on her face. She is so gonna give us all a run for our money in these next few years. I'm excited to watch her grow up into a badass woman. No, not just watch. I'm excited to help her grow up. It will be the honor of my life.

"Alright, kid. Whatcha got?"

Chapter Twenty-One

Griffin

"YOU LOOK LIKE SHIT," Bailey says as I open the door to let him in. I roll my eyes exaggeratedly at him and step back to let him into the house. Nessa took the kids out for dinner since, according to Amelia, I'm still "too sad to be around." She's probably right.

It's been almost a week since everything blew up, and other than a single text, I haven't heard from Cass. Amelia told me yesterday afternoon that Cass is back at the Songbird, but she didn't say much more. I caught her studying me with a calculating look, though. I was too tired to try to decipher it.

"What are you doing here, Bail?" I ask, exhausted.

"I've come to collect you for open mic night. Go get cleaned up."

"I don't know, man. What if Cass doesn't want to see me yet? I don't want to push her away any more than I already have."

"What the fuck are you talking about?" He stares at me with a puzzled look on his face, and I huff in frustration.

"The whole blow-up only happened with the kids because I was relying on her too much to hang out with the kids. I was busy acting like we were a happy family and didn't pay attention to the signs that it was too much for her."

"Dude. I really don't think it was about you or the kids. I think this had everything to do with her evil mother. Now, come on and get ready to go. I've been instructed to bring you to the open mic night at a certain time. I will not be angering my pregnant wife right before I leave for spring training." He raises his eyebrows at me, and I finally understand the girls have something planned. Hope lights in my chest. Maybe Cass is ready to see me after all.

"What are they planning? What do you know?"

"Nothing I'm allowed to tell you about." He shoots me a wink and tilts his head toward the stairs. "Now, I suggest you get a move on and make yourself presentable. We're on a schedule."

I chuckle and shake my head before racing for the stairs. I clean up the edges of my beard and take the world's fastest shower before throwing on jeans and a dark green Henley to bring out the green in my eyes. I do my best to tame my hair that's gotten too long. There's nothing I can do about the dark circles under my eyes, but hopefully I'll be sleeping much better tonight.

I'm back down the stairs in record time, grabbing my coat.

"Better?" I ask Bailey snarkily.

"Much," he says with a smirk. "I couldn't take you in public the way you were."

I roll my eyes, but he's not wrong. I didn't have any meetings yesterday and today, so I hadn't showered or changed out of my sweats. Actually, I'm really glad Cass didn't end up seeing me like that.

Bailey pats me on the shoulder and heads toward the front door.

"Let's go see our women, big brother."

"Right behind you, little brother."

BAILEY STOPS ME WITH a hand on my shoulder just before I'm about to open the door to the Songbird. I can tell without opening the door that Fred is on the stage. His voice is belting out Shaggy and Rik Rok's "It Wasn't Me," but he's definitely singing both parts himself. I chuckle to myself and raise my eyebrows at Bailey, who sticks his head inside the door.

He turns back to me to let me in the door. Sure enough, Fred is wearing a purple jacket and a gold ascot similar to what Shaggy wears in the music video. I shake my head, laughing as he hip-thrusts his way through the end of the song. Bailey leads us to a table near the front where Eric and Dan are already sitting and points at me to sit down.

I greet the guys and take my seat. I scan the room, but I don't see any of the girls. They are definitely plotting something. Bailey comes back with a beer for both of us and sits down.

Once Fred is done with his "Pop2K" flashback, he turns and arranges the microphones on the stage. He leaves one up front and center, but puts two more a few steps back and off to either side. I'm one hundred percent sure he's in on whatever the girls have planned.

As soon as Fred leaves the stage, the girls come filing out of the kitchen to cheers. They're all wearing togas that I'm almost certain are made of bedsheets. To my surprise, after Leena, Annie, and Jessie make their way out, my daughter and my ex-wife file in. *What the fuck?* Before I can ask

Bailey what's happening, Drew plops into the seat next to mine, having popped out of the kitchen with the ladies.

"Hi, Dad!"

"Hey, kiddo. What's going on?"

"I don't know," he says with a shrug. "But Mom and Cass said I can have a root beer float after the songs."

I laugh and ruffle his hair. And then I see her.

Cass is wearing a flowing purple dress with draped straps and a bodice that clings to her hips in all the right places. It has the same sort of Greek vibe the other ladies were going for with their bed sheet togas. She looks stunning. She meets my eyes almost immediately and offers me a soft smile that warms every part of my body.

She makes her way to the center microphone while the other five ladies group around the back two microphones. Leena hits something on her phone, and background music starts for just a second before Cass and the girls launch into "I Won't Say (I'm In Love)" from Disney's *Hercules*.

They've clearly practiced it because the girls singing the parts of the muses have a whole dance routine they're doing. I'm enjoying the number when the words Cass is singing hit me like lightning. The whole point of the song is that she *is in* love.

Is she trying to tell me something?

My heart rate kicks up even more when Cass moves to the piano and starts playing a slowed-down version of "Honey" by Taylor Swift. When she winks at me after the line about being a "forever night stand," I think my heart stops for a second.

She's definitely trying to tell me something. In the handful of times I slipped and called her honey, she never mentioned it. Never brought it up. I half-expected her to demand I stop using it. This is confirmation she liked the sweeter nickname, after all. Spitfire came so naturally from the beginning, but honey fits her just as much. Sweet once you break through her tough shell.

When she finishes the song, she motions with her head to meet her upstairs in the apartment. I nod and turn to Nessa to make sure she's got the kids, but she's already smiling at me.

"Go get her, Griff. The kids and I decided we'd give a school night sleepover at Mom's a try."

"Are you sure, Ness?"

"Definitely. Things are calming down at work. We should be able to do a more evenly split schedule soon, so this will be a good test run."

"Thanks, Nessa. For everything."

I give both of the kids a goodnight hug and say quick goodbyes to everyone else before finally following Cass to her apartment. I knock lightly on the door, and she opens it immediately, like she was waiting on the other side for me to knock.

I'm pleased to see she's changed into sweatpants and one of my shirts. The dress she wore downstairs was gorgeous, but seeing her in my clothes gives my inner caveman's ego a boost.

She steps back to let me in, and rather than moving past her into the room, I gather her in my arms instead. She melts into me, wrapping her arms around my waist and burying her face in my chest. I kick the door shut behind us and, without breaking our embrace, pull her over to the small loveseat so we can sit.

She stays curled up against me for a long moment, and when she pulls away, I find tears streaming down her face. I swipe them away. "Don't cry, honey."

She smiles. "I can't help it. I think your kids broke me."

"What do you mean?"

"Well, between Amelia telling me she needs me and begging me not to leave again and Drew latching onto me the second he saw me and not letting go for a full minute, I think they've completely broken through any walls I used to have. All the emotions are coming through full blast now."

I smile down at the brave woman in my arms, somehow falling even more in love with her. "I don't see a problem."

"Neither do I, but I owe you some explanation."

"You don't have to—"

"Yes, I do. I want to. I want you to know everything about why I've been so closed off." I nod and sit back in my seat. She drops her gaze to her hands, takes a deep breath, then looks back into my eyes.

"My earliest memories of my mom are of her pinching me when I wasn't sitting still enough or quiet enough in church. Not playful, mind-your-manners pinches, but ones that left bruises."

I swallow hard, doing my best to tamp down the rage I already feel for her mother.

"As I got older, it escalated to slaps, especially if I talked back or had less than perfect grades.

"It wasn't just physical, though. Every word she spoke was a constant critique. I wasn't pretty enough, smart enough, or thin enough. No one would ever love me the way I was. In middle school, when I was on the heavier side, before I had my growth spurt, she put me on diets that were basically starvation-level. If she wanted to punish me, she'd take away meals.

"My mom always acted like she was doing what was best for me. She told me often how she had given up everything to have me. She'd remind me how ungrateful I was. She had been a model before she got pregnant with me and had to stop once she started showing. My own mother reminded me all the time how I was unlovable."

She pauses her explanation to swipe tears from her face, and I can't help but ask, "Where was your dad in all this?" There's no world where I would let someone treat my kids this way, not even their mother.

"He tried to shield me when he could, but for the most part, he'd keep his head down and let it happen. She was just as horrible to him, maybe worse, behind closed doors. When they got divorced, he didn't take me with him, and I was left alone with her from thirteen to eighteen. It's why I wasn't on good terms with him when he died. I always thought maybe we'd be able to have a relationship someday, but it didn't happen. I went full no-contact with her after his funeral and had her number and all social media blocked until last week."

Cass grabs a tissue. She gives me a quick rundown of the phone call she got from her mother. My blood is still boiling, and I really hope I never meet this woman, because I am not well-suited for prison.

"It's no excuse. I never should have snapped at Drew. I'm so unbeliev-ably sorry. The second the words were out of my mouth, I was horrified, both that I hurt his feelings and because they were the exact words my mom had said hundreds of times when I was a kid. I heard her voice coming out of my mouth, and I panicked. I was afraid I would be just like her, and I refused to break Amelia and Drew the way she broke me. So, I called Leena, and I ran."

Cass cries harder, and I pull her into my chest. I drag my hand through her hair, doing my best to comfort her. When she finally calms a bit, I murmur, "You know you're not your mother, right?"

She sniffles and sits up again. "Yes. Thanks to Meg, Zander, Leena, and an emergency session with my therapist, I'm finally seeing there's no chance of me becoming my mother."

"Good. There's also no chance of me being like your dad. He's just as much to blame as your mom, as far as I'm concerned. I would never let my kids stay in a situation that was harming them. It's your one job as a parent, and I'm so sorry both of yours failed so spectacularly.

"You have been through so much, and it's no wonder you came through it closed off and guarded. What you had to survive conditioned you to protect yourself at all costs. You are so fucking brave, Cass."

She blinks at me for a moment. Then, like the sun breaking through the clouds on a rainy day, she gives me the brightest smile and says, "I love you."

I inhale sharply, and my nose stings with tears. I had half convinced myself I would never hear those words from her. That I would live forever, afraid to tell her the full truth of how I feel. I can't resist crashing my lips into hers, drawing a surprised squeak out of her. She melts into the kiss, and I could stay there forever, but I pull away to say, "I love you, too. I think I've loved you since the moment you spilled water on me. The moment I saw you across the bar, I was drawn to you. I couldn't have resisted it if I tried."

She lets out a garbled laugh. "I think I knew then, too. It's why I shut down any chance of finding each other again. I was so scared of letting anyone in, and I knew you'd break down my walls."

"I'll spend forever breaking through every wall you've built around your heart. I get why you built them, but I'll never stop working to earn my place inside."

"The kids definitely helped your case. I fought hard against the chemistry between you and me, fought against loving you, but the kids slipped into my heart without trying."

I laugh and take her lips again, tilting her head back to deepen the kiss. "Still think I'm a walking complication?" I ask as I move to kissing her jaw and down her neck.

She chuckles low and pulls me by the hand toward the bed across the room, shedding my shirt as she goes. She slides the sweatpants down to reveal nothing underneath. My gaze travels down her body. She perches herself on the edge of her bed and reaches for me. Our eyes lock as she answers my question.

"Turns out I like things a little complicated."

Epilogue

Cass

Six Months Later

"I THINK THIS IS the last box," Griffin says as he sets a random box of kitchen stuff onto the countertop in our kitchen. "You're officially moved in!"

I roll my eyes and laugh. I haven't actually lived in the Songbird apartment for months, but I hadn't cleared out all of my stuff until now. The last time I even camped out there for the night was probably a couple of months ago, now that Alaina's moved to full time and we hired two more bartenders/baristas.

With Leena being out on maternity leave, and the bar team growing, I hadn't had a spare minute to think about packing up random shit in the apartment. I'm only doing it now because we've decided to turn the apartment into office space and a break room for the team.

"Okay, I'm gonna get cleaned up for open mic. Care to join me in the shower?" Griffin's eyes go dark as he pushes off the counter he was leaning on. "We can practice our song for tonight."

He stops in his tracks and groans. "Ugh, don't remind me. I don't understand why I have to sing?"

I move to stand in front of him, looping my arms around his neck. "You're the only one in our friend group who hasn't performed during open mic. Even your parents sang a duet last month. It's basically a rite of passage." He grumbles under his breath. "Plus, it's our song, and I gave you the slower part."

He rests his hands on my hips and wiggles me from side to side. "I still say our song is 'Hips Don't Lie' since it's the first song we danced to." He swivels my hips, making me laugh again.

"Okay, you might be right. But 'Hips Don't Lie' isn't as fun to sing for open mic as 'Free' is. Plus, the lyrics made me think of you the first time we watched *K-Pop Demon Hunters*." I trail my hand down his chest and start unbuttoning the short-sleeved button-down he has on. "Besides, I'll make it worth your while."

He swallows, eyes following my hands as they make their way down to the front of his shorts. "And how will you do that?"

"Join me in the shower and find out," I say as I strip my shirt over my head. I toss it into his face and take off running for the shower in our room.

He catches me quickly, and I let out a scream as he scoops me off the ground and carries me the rest of the way to the bathroom. He drops me onto my feet in front of the shower and makes quick work of getting the water going while I strip out of my shorts, bra, and underwear. Griffin strips down, too, and we hurry into the shower.

I gasp at the water that's still too cold, but the heat of Griffin behind me makes me forget the water temperature quickly. Before I can spin around, his hands are reaching around my body. His hands find my nipples and give them a sharp tweak, making me hiss and grind my ass back into his already very hard dick.

With one hand, he grips my hip, holding me to him, and the other hand presses in the center of my back, bending me over.

"Put your hands on the wall, Spitfire," Griffin growls, and I move quickly to obey, already trembling with anticipation.

In a move that surprises me, he lets go of me to reach for the hand-held shower head. When I try to peek up to see what he's doing, he just presses me back into my bent-over position. He brings the shower head across my nipples, and I notice he's adjusted the spray so it's a concentrated stream.

I moan as the powerful blast of warm water hits my nipples, my body tensing as I realize where he's going with this. He travels the water down my stomach, then reaches his other hand around to cup my pussy. He runs a finger up my slit and uses his hand to hold me open so he can train the water stream directly against my clit.

My hips buck, trying to get away from the intensity of the water, but his hard body has me boxed in. He leans forward to growl into my ear, "I'm gonna make you come so hard with just this stream of water, and then when you're screaming and clenching around nothing, I'm gonna fill you up while you're still coming."

"Oh, fuck," I whimper, dropping my head to hang between my hands. The intense and unrelenting pressure of the water has my legs shaking in seconds, and before I know it, my orgasm is crashing into me.

Griffin does exactly what he promised. As my body tenses and I writhe against him, he notches himself at my entrance and slides in with one powerful thrust that intensifies and prolongs my release.

"That's it, Spitfire. You're so fucking tight when you're already coming. Squeeze me so I can fill you with my cum. I want you to feel me dripping out of you when we're on stage later."

I have no idea if I'm having one long orgasm or several smaller ones back to back, but the waves of pleasure and euphoria don't recede as he pumps inside of me. Finally, he stills and comes on a long groan.

He drops his head to rest on my shoulder while he catches his breath and lowers the shower head away from my body. We're both breathing hard as he pulls out and resets the shower head to its normal setting, putting it back on the holder so the water is cascading onto us.

I turn into Griffin's arms and rest my head on his chest, still trying to catch my breath. "I think you killed me," I murmur into his chest.

He chuckles low and runs his hands through my wet hair. "I think I killed us both. Guess we'll have to skip open mic."

I pinch his side. "Nice try. It's Leena's first open mic after having Jamie. Your parents have the baby. Our kids are at Nessa's for the weekend. We're going."

He huffs a laugh but doesn't argue. We wash quickly, both still recovering from the incredible shower sex.

We make a stop at Bibibop to grab some dinner before we head over to the Songbird. As we cross into the already full bar, a sense of pride comes over me. The place is packed with happy-looking people waiting for the open mic to begin. This place is mine. It's always felt like it, but now as a part owner, the pride and joy I feel being here is so fulfilling, it's borderline overwhelming.

We make our way over to where our friends have pushed two of the tables near the front together. Bailey may have been joking about there being a "Sisterhood of the Songbird Apartment," but you can't argue with the fact that all four of us who lived there are now in happy, healthy relationships.

Leena and Bailey are married with a newborn; nothing fake about their relationship now. Annie and Eric own a business together instead of hating each other, and I have it on good authority, he'll be proposing in the near future. Jessie and Dan brought their relationship back from the brink of divorce, and now she's due in December with baby number two, despite Lottie only being nine months old.

Then there's Griffin and me. I thought I was too broken for this life. I did my best to build up walls and armor to keep everyone out until Griffin and his kids blasted their way in. Thank God they did.

I'll never stop being grateful for this man. For his persistence. I could have missed out on the most beautiful life.

And I'll never stop being grateful for this place.

I owe everything to the Songbird Café.

The End

Thank you for reading The Chemistry Complication! Want more Cass & Griffin? Scan here for a free bonus epilogue!

Curious about any of the music found in *The Chemistry Complication*? Checkout this playlist to find all of the songs mentioned as well as a few extras!

Next Up

We're moving to the small town of Beachville Springs for Meg's single mom, love after loss story.
State of Grace coming Spring 2026!
Turn the page for a sneak peek!

(Excerpt subject to change)

State of Grace

Chapter One

Hunter

MY DAD IS AN evil genius, emphasis on evil. I mop the sweat from my brow before returning the hard hat to my soaked head. Gone are the days of sitting in my glass-walled office wearing a three-thousand-dollar bespoke suit, sipping a complicated latte handmade by my assistant, Helen. I sigh for the millionth time today, a trickle of sweat rolling between my shoulder blades.

My dad would say that I brought this on myself with my poor judgment, but I'm not sure I deserved this. Sure, I made a stupid mistake. I trusted the wrong person. I get why Dad was pissed after the incident. But this banishment to middle-of-fucking-nowhere-Ohio, to work on the ground crew installing fiber optic internet cables, is a low blow. Beachville Springs. What kind of fucking name is that for a town?

I'm supposed to be the next CEO of Morgan Communications, the telecommunication empire my great-grandfather founded before the internet was a thing. MC, as I like to call it to save on syllables, started as a utilities company, buying smaller electric and phone companies until the tech boom of the nineties turned it into the massive corporation it is today.

And I'm supposed to run the whole thing when my dad retires. Instead, I'm digging holes.

I chug a drink of water and head back to where the crew is running the lines. At least I'm acting as a supervisor and not the one down in the hole. Thank god for small miracles, I guess. The downside of being in charge here is I'm the one the busybodies in this town complain to about the holes in their yards. I've had four complaints today alone, and I might scream if I get any more.

As if I summoned the attention, a light, feminine voice behind me says, "Excuse me?" I sigh and pinch the bridge of my nose. I pretend not to hear her, but she repeats more firmly. "Excuse me."

"If you have complaints about our process, you should have received a flyer before the work started. There's a number you can call. It's not my fucking problem," I grumble without even turning to look.

"Hey!" she snaps harshly, and I finally turn around, annoyed, only to freeze at the sight of her.

The first thing I see is her wild blonde curls that seem to have a life of their own, spiraling in all directions in a cloud around her head. It reminds me of the illustrations in a mythology book I had growing up. That hair would fit right perfectly on a forest nymph or demigoddess.

Next, I find her curvy body. She's not short exactly, but she's not tall either, especially compared with my six-two height, and she has curves in all the right places. My eyes track down her body. At my perusal, she crosses her arms across her chest, which only serves to push up her incredible tits.

Finally, I drag my gaze up and zero in on her startling blue eyes, narrowed in fury. Maybe a gorgon would be the better comparison, since her furious gaze seems to have turned me to stone where I stand.

She huffs an angry breath. "I was trying to tell you that there's a cooler with cold water, Gatorades, and protein bars for you and your guys on my porch. Feel free to help yourselves."

"Oh, I—"

"I'd also appreciate it if you watched your fucking mouth in front of my kid," she snaps.

My gaze drops from the beauty in front of me to find a small boy standing next to her. He has her blue eyes, but his hair is straight and a light sandy brown. He looks up at her and tugs on her arm.

"Mom, swear jar!" he says, excitedly. "You said the F word, Mom!"

She sighs and rolls her eyes. "I was making a point, bud."

I close the distance between us and crouch in front of the kid. "How much does she owe for the F bomb, kiddo?"

"A dollar!" he shouts, jumping up and down.

I grab my wallet out of my back pocket. I bite down on my tongue when I realize the smallest bill I have is a fifty. Oh, well. I'm already in too far to stop. "Any chance you have change?" He scrunches his nose in confusion. "Eh, that's okay, buddy. Here, this will cover my slip and your mom's and give you some extra funding to work with."

His little eyes go wide at the sight of the fifty-dollar bill I hand him. His mom gasps as she realizes how much I gave him. "You don't need to—"

"Yes, I do." My eyes find hers, and the fury in them has dulled to suspicion. "I'm sorry for the language. It's been a frustrating day.

She hums in response and drops her arms, placing her hands on her fabulously curvy hips. I glance at her left hand to check for wedding rings, and I'm pleasantly surprised to find her hand bare. I hold my own hand out to her. "I'm Hunter Morgan."

There's no sign of recognition of my name, so it's possible that the tabloid garbage didn't reach small-town Ohio. She eyes my hand for a beat, I can almost see the temptation to leave me hanging cross her face before she reaches out and places her delicate hand in my larger one. "Meg Thompson," she says curtly.

A jolt of electricity races up my arm at the touch. Our eyes lock, and our hands stay linked a moment longer than necessary before she pulls back and clears her throat. I'd be willing to bet a lot of money that she felt the same spark I did.

"Anyway, we have to go, but tell your team about the cooler." She raises her eyebrows in question.

"Of course. Thank you."

She throws me a curt nod before ushering the kid to the newer-looking blue SUV parked in the driveway. She helps him buckle into a car seat, but glances back at me after shutting his door. I give her a wave and put my most charming smile on my face, which only makes her frown in response. Her brow furrows, and she shakes her head as she climbs into the SUV and backs out of the driveway.

"You piss off the homeowner, boss?" Stan, the project manager for the fiber install, asks suddenly behind me.

"Only a little. I think I fixed it. She left water for the crew in the cooler on her porch."

"Aw yeah, I fucking love small towns. So neighborly."

I chuckle. "Tell the guys to get some water and get back to work, Stan."

He grins my way and takes off toward the crew digging. "You got it, boss."

I shake my head and follow him. I throw myself back into work, but my mind is firmly on a pair of sparkling blue eyes and an electricity I've never felt before.

***

A few days later, I'm clomping my way across the front walk to my small rental house when my next-door neighbor and landlady, Mrs. Doris, shouts from her porch. "Mr. Morgan, do you have a minute?"

I sigh, not really wanting to chat but unable to say no to the older lady. I cross my small yard and part of hers to get to her front walk. She's sitting in a cushioned rocking chair on one side of a small table. A large pitcher of lemonade perched at the center of the table, condensation rolling down the outside of the glass.

"Lemonade?" she asks in a tone that tells me it wasn't really a question.

"That would be lovely, Mrs. Doris. And you can call me Hunter."

"Hunter. How was work today?"

"Very hot."

She chuckles. "I can see that," she points to the sweat still running down the side of my face. My drive wasn't long enough for the air conditioning in my truck to do much. This lemonade looks refreshing as hell.

Living next to Mrs. Doris might not be so bad. "Well, I have a favor to ask, and luckily it will be a much cooler project."

Spoke too soon. I freeze with my lemonade glass halfway to my mouth. I should have known this was a trap. "What's the favor?"

"My dear friend Margaret needs help with her creek clean-up project tomorrow morning. She only has a couple of people signed up. She could use a strapping young man like you." Mrs. Doris smirks and shoots me a conspiratorial look. "In more ways than one."

I study the older woman for a long moment. Her white hair is curled perfectly despite the heat, and her dark brown skin is flawless. She's doing her best to keep her expression innocent, but I can see the mischief twinkling in her eyes. "Am I helping with creek clean up, or are you trying to set me up with this friend of yours?"

"Let's just focus on it being a favor to me, young man. If you happen to hit it off with Margaret, then all the better." I narrow my eyes at Mrs. Doris, who gives me a serene smile. "I'd help her myself, but these old knees can't quite navigate the creek like they used to."

Mrs. Doris reminds me so strongly of my Nanny Rosa that I groan and tip my head back against my hair. There's no way I'll be able to say no. To help at the creek, that is. "I'm not dating your friend, Mrs. Doris."

She laughs. "We'll see about that, my boy. We'll see." I roll my eyes and shake my head, chugging down the rest of my lemonade. "They're meeting at the park pavilion at nine. You know where that is, right?"

I nod. "It's a pretty small town, Mrs. Doris. I think I've seen everything in the week I've been in town."

"Oh, I doubt that," she says with a smirk. "You've only seen the surface of what Beachville Springs has to offer. Luckily, Margaret will be a lovely tour guide for you."

I do my best not to roll my eyes at her. I don't need a tour guide or to be set up with some middle-aged small-town divorcée. "I'm not gonna be here that long, Mrs. Doris."

She eyes me with a skeptical stare. I really should have said, I'm hoping I'm not gonna be here that long. I'm in this podunk town until my dad calls me back to New York. Running fiber through this entire area is supposed to take close to a year. He wouldn't make me stay the whole time, right? I try not to think about the answer.

Mrs. Doris is still studying me over her lemonade glass, waiting for me to answer her about the creek cleanup. I blow out a big breath, giving up. "Fine. I'll help with the creek, but that's it."

"Lovely. I'll let Margaret know that she'll have an extra volunteer." She shoots me a triumphant smile.

I finish my lemonade and stand. "I'm gonna get out of here before you rope me into more town activities. Have a nice night, Mrs. Doris." I walk away before she can respond.

She laughs and calls after me. "You can run, but you can't hide, Mr. Morgan."

I scoff and shake my head. I believe her. I'm gonna be dodging her efforts to fold me into this town for the foreseeable future.

The next morning, I roll up to the park pavilion to find a group of about ten people. Short on volunteers, my ass. I'm tempted to drive away until I catch sight of a familiar head of curly blonde hair.

Today she's dressed in a pair of tight black spandex bike shorts that cling to her hips like a second skin and a bright pink athletic tank top. Tall, colorful rain boots are on her feet, and she's holding a clipboard, work gloves already on her hands. Her golden curls are pulled into a messy bun at the top of her head, but look like they may try to escape the tie at a moment's notice.

There's no chance of my driving away now. Not when she's here. I wasn't sure I'd see Meg again. We finished work on her street, so there was no reason for me to go back, but I'd hoped I would run into her. I should have known she'd be here.

Regretting the ratty tee shirt and gym shorts I threw on this morning, I run my hand through my hair and check my reflection in the rear-view mirror. I didn't bother shaving before I left the house, not wanting to give Mrs. Doris's setup the wrong idea. I grab a baseball hat that I left in the truck last week and resign myself to a less-than-perfect second impression. Can't be that much worse than my first impression of snapping at her and swearing in front of her kid.

Fuck.

I approach the group, offering an awkward wave before shoving my hands into my shorts pockets. Meg's eyes widen as she recognizes me, and her gaze rakes up and down my body, taking in my old, grungy workout clothes. My cheeks heat with embarrassment under her perusal, and I nervously yank my hat off my head, putting it back on backwards.

"What on earth are you doing here?"

Chapter Two

Meg

The words fly out of my mouth without my permission. I sound unbelievably bitchy, but I'm thrown off by the hot worker guy's appearance at our creek cleanup. Hunter. His name is burned into my brain from the startling wave of electricity that came over me when I shook his hand in my yard earlier this week.

Even now, with him standing six feet away from me, there's a change in the atmosphere, like the part of my nervous system that had been lying dormant is now wide awake. I frown, not sure how I feel about the sensation.

I step away from my group of volunteers. The gossip will already be flying after I just snapped at a perfect stranger. I don't need to give them any more to work with. His brow furrows at my harsh question, cheeks turning pink, with embarrassment or frustration, I'm not sure.

"Um, Mrs. Doris sent me," he says. He clears his throat and shuffles his feet a bit.

"Mrs. Doris?" The connection finally dawns on me. "You're her new tenant."

I pinch the bridge of my nose. Mrs. Doris has been campaigning for me to meet her new tenant since he moved in a few weeks ago. I should have known a meddler like her wouldn't take no for an answer.

"That's me. Did she tell you I was coming?"

"Nope." I decide not to elaborate on Mrs. Doris's matchmaking scheme. "You know we're cleaning the creek, right? You're gonna get your fancy sneakers all wet and muddy."

I point to his expensive-looking running shoes. He glances down and shrugs.

"These are about shot for running. I already have a new pair. Shouldn't be an issue."

I shake my head and shrug. "Okay, man."

"Hunter." He smirks, dipping his head to meet my eye, and a swarm of butterflies takes off in my stomach.

"Right."

"And you're Meg, right?" I watch as realization flickers across his face. "Or wait, shit, are you Margaret?"

"Goddammit, Mrs. Doris," I grumble, half under my breath. Hunter laughs, a deep, pleasant sound, and the butterflies pick up again. Fucking hell. "Nobody calls me Margaret but Mrs. Doris."

"Got it. Meg." He nods and shoots me a cocky smile. This guy knows exactly how attractive he is, and it's clear Mrs. Doris already briefed him on her matchmaking efforts based on the way he's looking at me.

I roll my eyes and turn back to the creek cleanup crew, determined to focus on the reason we're here and not the gorgeous man beside me.

"Alright, y'all, we're gonna start at the bridge and work north to the access road. I've got buckets, gloves, and trash bags over here. Let me know if you have any questions." I smile at the group of volunteers. Several of them have been creek cleaning with me before, and thanks to living in such a small town, I know each of them by name.

They jump to grab supplies, and Hunter follows suit, falling in line beside me as we walk toward the trail that will lead us to the creek. Side conversations pick up around us, but I keep my eyes down on the trail ahead of me.

Hunter clears his throat. "Do you always run the creek cleanups?"

"Mostly. I'm pretty involved around town."

Sarah Collins, owner of Mix'n'Match, a self-serve frozen yogurt shop, and my best friend in town, lets out a loud snort on the other side of me. "That's an understatement. Meg practically runs this town."

I shoot her a glare and shake my head. "Hardly. I have plenty of time, I might as well be helping out." Sarah scoffs again but doesn't add more.

"Mrs. Doris said you'd be the best tour guide for me as I get to know the town."

Before I can shut down the idea, Sarah pipes up again. "Oh, definitely. Meg knows everyone and is on most of the town committees." I catch her eye to telepathically tell her to shut the fuck up, but she just smirks back at me. She's right around my age and has been subjected to Mrs. Doris's matchmaking efforts as much as I have. She's clearly joining Team Mrs. Doris on this one.

Hunter's mouth opens, but I'm saved by George Sanderson, the hardware store owner who looks like Santa Claus year-round, calling out from up ahead, "Meg, where's Beckett today? I'm missing my bucket-holding buddy."

I grin at George, my mind flashing to all the creek cleanups I've brought Beckett to this summer. "He's with Lydia. I believe they were baking a cake for Gavin's birthday dinner tomorrow." I mentally congratulate myself for not stammering over any of the words in the sentence despite the pang of grief they cause in my chest.

George and Sarah both shoot me sympathetic glances, and I risk a look at Hunter. He looks puzzled, like he has no idea what we're talking about, but I don't see the familiar pity showing on his face. Mrs. Doris must not have given him a full history.

Luckily, we arrive at the creek, and I can focus on picking up trash left behind by hikers and tourists instead of the magnetic new guy in town. Mrs. Doris seems so hell-bent on setting me up with Hunter. Am I even ready to be set up? It's been three years, and some days, when I'm particularly lonely, I think I could be. But other days, the grief sits so solidly in the front of my mind, I couldn't possibly think about moving on.

I keep my head down and focus on sifting through leaves and twigs to find food wrappers and water bottles. After working for about an hour, a laughing shout from Hunter catches my attention. I splash over to where he's been working to find him holding up a pair of large underwear.

I chuckle. "That's a new one."

He huffs a laugh as he turns to me. "I have so many questions."

"We always find weird stuff."

"But like, who loses underwear in a creek? Did they wear these to the creek and forget them? What were they wearing when they left?" He's laughing as he asks his series of questions, mirth dancing in his dark brown eyes.

"I don't think I want to know the answers to any of those questions."

He throws the underwear in his trash bag and shakes his head. I linger nearby instead of going back to the other side of the creek.

"You just moved to town, right?"

He nods. "Yeah, I'm here to supervise the fiber optic cable install. We're doing the entire town, so it's gonna take a while. Most of the guys on the crew are from around here, but I live in New York."

"So you're not here permanently?"

"Nah, eventually I'll head back to the city." I nod and pick up a gray plastic grocery bag. "What about you? How long have you lived in Beachville Springs?"

I do my best to ignore the pang of disappointment that he's only here temporarily. Why do I even care? I answer simply, "I moved here after college." Not sure I want to explain Gavin to him if Mrs. Doris didn't. Not today.

I'm saved from elaborating by a scrap of white cloth spotted out of the corner of my eye. Just as I suspected, it's another enormous pair of underwear. I hold the soggy drawers out at arm's length. "Look what I found. The plot thickens."

"You've got to be fucking kidding me. Another pair?" Hunter laughs and holds open his trash bag in front of me. "I don't know if this makes it better or worse."

"Me neither."

We stand grinning for a long moment, our eyes locking, the atmosphere between us stilling. My stomach drops like I'm at the top of a roller coaster. What is it about Hunter that affects me so much? Why do I kind of like it?

I clear my throat and keep moving along the creek bed, willing the blush in my cheeks to fade. Hunter walks alongside me, and I can feel his gaze on me. We continue in comfortable quiet, the only sounds the splash of our feet in the creek and the rest of the team's chatter up ahead.

Over the next half hour, we find four more pairs of underwear, laughing harder with each pair we unearth in the creek. Hunter starts speculating on the scenarios that would cause six pairs of underwear to be left behind.

"Do you think someone was doing laundry in the creek?" I ask.

"That doesn't explain why they were all so spread out."

"True. The real question is if they all belonged to one person or if six people separately lost their undies here."

We both crack up, and I have to cross my legs to keep from peeing my pants, thanks to the nine-pound Beckett that ruined my pelvic floor muscles five years ago. It's the hardest I've laughed in a very long time.

Hunter's cheeks are pink with the heat of the day and our collective hysteria. Our gazes lock again, and the butterflies that have been plaguing me all morning pick up the pace again.

He takes a step toward me, stepping within arm's reach. "Could we—"

A loud alarm from my phone in the pocket of my shorts interrupts whatever Hunter was going to say. I tap my watch to turn off the alarm and take a step back.

"It's time to head back," I call out so our whole group can hear me. I sneak a glance at Hunter to find his eyes still on me. "I've gotta get back to get Beckett."

"Right, yeah." He nods, and we turn back the way we came, moving a little more quickly.

I make small talk with Sarah as we walk back, instead of Hunter, even though he walks quietly with us. I desperately want to know what he was about to say before my alarm interrupted us, but I'm also afraid to know. If he asks me out, I have no idea what I'll say. I shake my head hard to get rid of the thought. I'm getting way ahead of myself here.

"You okay?" Sarah asks quietly.

"Yeah, I'm good," I say too casually.

"You know it's okay, if you're not okay. There's no wrong timeline for these things."

"I know, thanks." I give her a tight smile and squeeze her hand. We're both still wearing our work gloves, but the contact makes me feel a little better. A little less alone.

I risk a peek at Hunter, and his brow is furrowed like he's trying to figure out a puzzle. When he notices me looking at him, his expression clears, and he gives me a soft smile. I surprise myself by smiling back at him, feeling lighter than I have in years.

What the fuck?

Back in the parking lot, we consolidate the trash, placing it in one of the park bins. Everyone helps to load the extra supplies into the back of my SUV. Most of the group makes sure to give me a sympathetic pat on the arm or a pitying smile as they leave, bringing today's date back into focus.

Hunter hangs back so that he's the last one standing with me at the back of my car. He tosses his work gloves on the pile and runs a hand through his sweaty hair before putting his hat back on backwards. A tug of heat I haven't felt in a long time hits me low in my gut at the sight of him. He really is a gorgeous guy.

"So, I know Mrs. Doris offered you up as a tour guide, but I was hoping..." His voice trails off as I reach up to fix my hair with my left hand. His eyes follow the path of my hand and widen at the sight of the wedding set I forgot I put on this morning. "Oh. I thought... Mrs. Doris... I'm sorry, I didn't realize you were married. I should—"

"Hunter," I interrupt his rambling apologies. "I was married, past tense. I, um..." I drag in a deep breath, preparing to level with him. "I wear my rings on bigger days as a way to remember, I guess? Today is my late husband's birthday. He would have been thirty-one, but he died in a car accident just over three years ago."

He stares at me, stunned a bit by my trauma dump. "Fuck. I'm so sorry."

"Thanks." I shrug and give him a sad smile. "It's a weird day."

"Shit. I bet."

An awkward tension hangs over us. Neither of us seems to know where to go from here. He fiddles with his hat a bit, and I make the executive decision to put us out of our misery.

"Well, I gotta head out and grab Beckett from my mother-in-law's house." I lower the hatch of my SUV and step toward the driver's side. Hunter backs toward his truck, which is parked a few spots down from mine.

"Right, yeah. I'll... It was good to see you again, Meg."

"You too, Hunter."

He gives me a smile and a nod before turning and walking to his truck. I watch him walk away for just a second before hopping in my car and driving out of the park.

I have a strong suspicion that he was going to ask me out before he spotted my rings. It makes sense that he backtracked. A kid is one thing, but the whole widow thing is a whole other layer of baggage, so I can't say I blame him. I understand it, but I can't quite shake the unexpected disappointment.

Maybe I'm more ready to move on than I thought.

Scan here to continue reading!

Acknowledgements

Wow! Book four and one whole year as a published author! This book officially wraps up my very first series and sometimes I'm still in shock that I was able to finish one book, let alone a full series of four. As someone who very likely has undiagnosed ADHD, I've tried (and discarded) many hobbies and creative outlets through the years, and none have been as rewarding as writing. I don't plan on stopping anytime soon!

As always, none of this would have been possible without the many wonderful people in my life who make the authoring possible.

First up, of course, is my awesome husband, Blair. You may not have read my books but you never fail to show up to support me in my authoring goals. I love you and this life we've built!

Thank you to my boys for spending many hours watching YouTube Kids while I try to write. I know it's a burden but you guys keep plugging away at that screen time. In all seriousness, Mommy loves you more than anything and hopes this paragraph is the only part of the book you've read!

Big shout out to my mama. Your help with the boys and being my constant sounding board keeps me sane. I love you and I'm so glad you live with us!

To Rachel, my ride or die bestie. I thanked you in the first set of acknowledgements of this series so I thought you should get another shout

out in the last! Thank you for being my un-biological sister for half of our lives so far!

To my dear childhood friend Drew, who we lost a few years ago after a courageous battle with colon cancer. I wrote the fictional Drew in this book to hold on to some of my favorite memories of you with your deep love of Peter Pan and musical theater. I can still vividly remember us singing together through the years. My books wouldn't have been your genre of choice but I know you would have been proud anyway. Twenty-nine years of friendship wasn't enough. I wanted more.

A huge thank you goes to my editor, Lily Luchesi at Partners In Crime Book Services. I love working with you and look forward to many more books together! Thank you for loving Cass as much as I do!

To the wonderful The Meighan PA for your amazing Promo Kit. Your promo work in reader groups has been indispensable for bringing new readers to my stories and I can't wait to continue working with you!

Thank you to my beta readers Abby, Kaitlin, Katie, and Mave for your incredibly valuable feedback.

Shout out to Girls On The Run which is a real non-profit empowerment program for girls in grades 3-8 that mixes training for a 5k with messages of confidence and self-worth. I served as a volunteer coach years ago (despite my distinct dislike for actual running) and the organization still has a big place in my heart.

Big thanks to @the.smut.daddy on Threads for inspiring me with her Star Wars rewatch so much that it made an appearance Chapter 11. My editor told me I shouldn't make such a specific reference but I couldn't stand the idea of cutting it so in it stayed.

Shout out to my author friends in the Nighttime Sprinters chat and the Author Accountability discord. I love having author besties to write with and learn from!

To my Fit4Mom Columbus North village and book club, you're all amazing and I couldn't do motherhood without you!

Thank you to Storyline Bookshop for not only being the first bookstore to carry my books but also for hosting a romance book club! I adore visiting my book babies on your shelf and yapping about other romance books every month!

Massive shout out to everyone involved in the Heated Rivalry fandom. Everyone from Rachel Reid, to the cast and crew of the show, to my many Loon friends on Threads deserve big thanks for their contributions to society as a whole and my own personal mental health!

Once again big love to BIGGBY Coffee and Taco Bell!

Finally, to you the reader, I owe my biggest thanks! Whether this was your first read of mine or you've been here from the beginning, I love each and every one of you and appreciate you so much!

xo, Maggie

Also by Maggie

The Songbird Cafe Series

The Songbird Setup (Leena & Bailey)

The Boss Boycott (Annie & Eric)

The Marriage Meltdown (Jessie & Dan)

The Chemistry Complication (Cass & Griffin)

Beachville Springs

State of Grace (Meg & Hunter)

About the Author

Maggie Linn Sharpe has been creating worlds and characters in her mind for as long as she can remember. Because no career path felt quite right, despite her efforts, and motherhood limited her social time, she decided to try writing a romance novel. Now she's pretty sure she won't be able to stop.

Maggie lives outside of Columbus, Ohio with her husband, her two boys, and her mother. When she's not writing, she's usually reading romance, obsessing about musicals, or spending time with her kiddos, which usually involves learning more than she wanted to know about Minecraft and watching Bluey on repeat.

Connect with Maggie